BERTIE'S BOOK OF SPOOKY WONDERS

OCELOT EMERSON

Month9Books

Copyright © 2019 by Ocelot Emerson

BERTIE'S BOOK OF SPOOKY WONDERS by Ocelot Emerson
All rights reserved. Published in the United States of America by Month9Books, LLC.
No part of this book may be used or reproduced in any manner whatsoever without written permission of the publisher, except in the case of brief quotations embodied in critical articles and reviews.

Trade Paperback ISBN: 978-1-948671-89-7
ePub ISBN: 978-1-948671-90-3
Mobipocket ISBN: 978-1-948671-91-0

Published by Tantrum Books for Month9Books, Raleigh, NC 27609

Cover illustration by Tatiana A. Makeeva.
Cover design by Danielle Doolittle

To my non-spooky nephews Jeremiah, Joseph, Samuel, and Tony, and my super-fantastic boys Han and Van.

PRAISE FOR *BERTIE'S BOOK OF SPOOKY WONDERS*

"A brilliant and highly entertaining [hilarious] story to help us all see what we've been missing and to live the life we were born to live. Kids, good luck getting this one back from your parents."—Mike Dooley, NY Times bestselling author of *Infinite Possibilities*

"101% Fantastic. *Bertie's Book of Spooky Wonders* leaps off the page like a great movie. Wildly funny and flawed hero. Heart wrenching story. Terrific twists. Bertie grabbed me from the opening chapter and never let go. Finding a pair of glasses that allows you to see a better version of yourself—sign me up. My kids too!"—Eric Blehm, NYT bestselling author of *Fearless*

"I would NEVER be allowed to get away with the stuff Bertie pulled! Can't wait to read the next one."—5th grader from Sanford, NC

"I liked this book and the characters. Bertie was funny and the farting dog reminded me of my weenier dog, Sampson."—4th grader from Portland, OR

BERTIE'S BOOK OF SPOOKY WONDERS

1

Two Wolves

I was dead.

Not literally, not dead-dead. I just told her, while gazing out my window at the bleak, dark, and unfamiliar surroundings, that I felt dead inside.

My mom said, "Remember when you insisted that I give you a heads-up if you got too morbid? Heads-up, kiddo."

"Don't you want to know why I feel this inner deadness?" I asked.

"Pretty sure I already do, Bertie," she said.

We had been driving for nine hours. Nearly all that time, Mom wore a freakish perma-smile. I sat beside her, Leon resting on my lap. My small and beloved and extremely lazy rescue dog farted so often, I practically needed a Hazmat suit.

"The reason I feel dead inside is because *someone* in this

car stole my life," I said, speaking to both Mom and Leon. "Now, I'm not the kind of girl who likes to name names, so I'll just look at the guilty party and whistle."

Gazing in Mom's direction, I gave her a quick whistle.

Still smiling, she said, "Grab a ticket, Leon, we are going on a guilt trip."

Ignoring Mom's comment, I kept talking. "And now everything about my amazing life as an adorably disagreeable girl growing up in a happy house with the perfect amount of friends, and a super-fantastic father, is deader than those bugs on our windshield. Which, by my count, is like one hundred."

SPLAT!

"Make that one hundred and one," I said as a giant dragonfly stuck itself to the windshield. I sighed dramatically, like a cruddy stage actress.

"Hate to break it to you, sweetheart, but no one can steal your happiness," Mom said. "But you can throw it away."

I groaned. Not at Mom's fortune cookie wisdom, but at the big green road sign up ahead: *Welcome to Altoona, Pennsylvania*. After an endless day of road travel, bad feelings, and stiff legs, Mom, Leon, and I had officially crossed over into our new, tangled-up, awful lives.

"When in doubt, Bertie, go for kindness," Mom said, as we drove through the city, just past eleven PM. "You'll make everyone's life easier, especially your own."

The odds were stacked against her on that one. I didn't feel like being kind. And I had zero interest in making anyone's life easier. I just wanted to go back home to Carver City, North Carolina. But it was five hundred and fifty-six miles in the wrong direction. I'd been watching our odometer turn and turn and turn.

Two years ago after my parents divorced, Mom and I became a package deal. Up until now we'd made it work. Mom didn't have my father's flamboyant style—he's a dashing attorney with a flair for courtroom theatrics he called his "Barcelona blood"—and she wasn't quite as much fun, but Mom was as solid and true as the Great Smoky Mountains. She made me her number one priority in all things. In her heart I know she thought this move would be good for both of us.

But she needed to think again.

Here are the distressing details of my mother's "fresh start" plan. Mom, Leon, and I were going to live with Mom's boyfriend, Howard Morton. Howard is an optometrist and a widower who lives with his two kids—Mac was eight, and Tabitha was my age, twelve—in Altoona. In September, when Mom and Howard got hitched, Howard would be my stepdad, and Tabitha and Mac would become my stepsister

3

and stepbrother.

The moment I learned of Mom's plan, I fought it with everything I had. Nothing worked. Not my threats to run away, nor my broccoli hunger strike, nor my crying fits whenever Mom said the words "fresh start" or "Howard Morton."

Bump-thump. Bumpity-thump-thump-thump.

Behind our station wagon we dragged a U-Haul trailer that threatened to disconnect from the hitch with each big bump in the road. In my mind it was a treasure chest of the life I left behind. Up ahead, headlights from oncoming cars cast my mom in a haunting mix of lights and shadows. It made her look like two different people.

Good mama.

Bad mama.

Good mama.

Bad mama.

And this is precisely when things turned from bad to spooky.

Check it out. Mom was driving a little too eagerly through the strange city streets, when a bizarre wave of dread shot up my spine and exploded into my brain. It's super important that you understand this was not the normal dread I had become accustomed to carrying around with me like my school backpack. No, this was mega-dread. Horror movie dread. I tried to ignore it, but I couldn't. It felt like someone was whispering in my ear that something horrible would happen. Now, no actual words were said, but I got the message loud and clear—we were driving toward disaster.

Hugging Leon tighter, I rubbed his velvety ears and mentally promised to protect him from whatever monsters were lurking in the dark. He had no reaction whatsoever. Leon isn't what you'd call an "emotional dog."

I wanted to warn my mom, but I stopped myself. She knew I didn't want to be in Pennsylvania, so she would never believe me. Plus, I wasn't exactly sure if I believed me.

"When I was your age, your great-aunt Tillie told me a legend about how we shape our fates," Mom said, switching to her softer storytelling voice. "According to the legend, every person is born with two wolves inside them."

"So that would mean I have two wolves inside me right now?" I said.

"Can I finish the story, please? Yes, you have two wolves inside you, and they are fighting to survive. One wolf is kind and loving and generous. The other wolf is mean and angry and selfish. The person you become, Bertie, depends upon which wolf you feed."

"You're done, right?" I asked, trying to keep fear out of my voice.

Mom nodded.

"Cool. It's a nice legend, Mom, but there's one problem. If I have two wolves inside me, I'm pretty sure I'll need to buy bigger pants …" Before I could finish my smart-aleck remark, Mom shouted a swear word she told me to never say, and cut the steering wheel hard to the right.

Through the windshield I spotted two huge dogs in the middle of the road looking straight at us. Wait, not dogs—wolves. One was grayish and white with icy diamond blue eyes, and the other was grayish and black with hot ruby red eyes. The wolves were big and scary and beautiful, and they were about to become fury road pizzas.

"AHHH!" Mom and I screamed.

Swerving just enough to miraculously avoid hitting the wolves, Mom skidded to a hard stop. We swapped terrified looks. When I looked back at the road, it was empty of wolves.

"Where'd they go?" I said, breathless. "How could they be gone already?"

Mom shook her head in shock. "How bizarre was that?"

"Beyond bizarre. Freaky bizarre! I mean, come on, you were talking about two wolves, and out of nowhere, *wham*, there were two wolves in the road."

"No, Bertie, those were not wolves. This is Pennsylvania. No wolves."

"Those were wolves, Mom!"

"They were probably Siberian Huskies. Those dogs look a lot like wolves."

"And the wolves in the road looked exactly like wolf-wolves," I protested.

"Yeah… maybe," Mom said, swallowing a jagged breath.

We sat in silence, gathering our bearings.

"Alright, I have no idea what just happened, but it happened, and it was freaky, and now it's over," Mom said, wanting me to feel safe. "Howard's house is only ten minutes from here, Bertie. I'll call and ask him if there are wolves in Altoona, okay?" She squeezed my hand and smiled.

"Okay, cool," I said, gripping her hand.

Neither of us realized the wolves were an omen.

And I didn't know the omen would launch a long parade of cosmic craziness that would forever change how I saw the world, or that my life was about to crack wide open like an egg falling onto the kitchen floor. If I had known the tragic details of the disaster coming my way, I would've done things differently. I would've found the courage to warn my mother. And I would've been a whole lot kinder to everyone involved.

Another wave of dread hit me as Mom pulled forward.

Another frozen whisper.

One last final warning.

Altoona is not a fresh start. It's the beginning of the end.

2

The Mortifying Mortons

"Remember, Bertie, you only get one chance to make a first impression," Mom said, after she parked in the gigantic driveway. "So don't blow it."

I still hadn't caught my breath. Mom had called Howard as promised, and he assured us there were no wolves in Pennsylvania. Naturally, that made me despise Howard even more. It was like the world was spinning out of control, and Mom couldn't see it. I was desperate to shout, "This is NOT a fresh start, Mom. Bad-bad stuff is about to go down!" But there was no way she would've heard me. She had been driving the last five hundred miles under the influence of great expectations.

When Mom opened the car door and stepped onto the pavement of Howard's driveway, she was glowing. Where

8

I was jam-packed with dread and nightmares, Mom was overflowing with hopes and dreams.

And just like that, I knew that our first impression was not going to go according to her plans. I was about to blow it—big time. It's like when an adult tells you to not cry before they tell you a sad story, and then they tell you the story and you cry anyway. Some things, like sad stories causing tears, and me screwing things up, are pretty much automatic.

During the long drive I made a solemn vow to loathe Howard Morton and anyone connected to him. So when the front door of the house flung open and Howard bumbled out, waving and smiling, I hated him immediately. I could not believe that my mother planned to marry that big bozo. Tabitha and her little brother, Mac, appeared next. They looked different now, in person, than they did during the video chats I was forced to endure when Mom and I lived in North Carolina. I hated them, too.

I crawled out of our car. Wanted to crawl back in and lock the doors.

Howard kissed my mom and gave her a tight hug. The tornado inside my gut spun faster. Howard let go of my mom and smiled at me. He patted me on the head. "Welcome to my house, Bernice, which is also your house now."

The tornado rose from my belly and into my throat. I *hate*

9

it when people call me Bernice, even though it's technically my legal name. Bernice is an old lady knitting socks in a rocking chair. Bertie, on the other hand, could be the name of a rock star or a movie star or even a musical prodigy. Someone way more spectacular than *Bernice*.

"Mr. Howard?" I said. "Since I believe honesty is the best policy, I got to say two things. One: There *are* wolves in Altoona. And two: Your house is definitely not my house."

"Bertie, that's so rude," Mom said, jabbing me with eye daggers. "Apologize to Howard this minute."

"Not necessary," Howard said, grinning and tossing an arm around Mom's shoulders. "First day jitters and all that. I'm good. Trust me, I have them too. And it's just Howard, Bernice, not Mr. Howard."

He said it again!

I wanted to accidentally stomp on Howard's foot. Instead, I fetched Leon from the car. That was when a chill passed through me and prickled my skin.

But it was worse than before. I felt a deep pang of loneliness that did not seem to be my own particular brand of loneliness, that heartache I got when I worried that everyone I loved would eventually abandon me like an unwanted dog or cat left on the side of a road. It hurt me, right down to my bones.

Have you ever seen a person at a store or some other place

who was oozing so much loneliness or sadness that some of the ooze splashed onto you, and you felt sad or lonely, too? It was that kind of situation. I felt like I had taken on someone else's loneliness, which did not make a lick of sense. The people around me were happy, it seemed.

When I thought things couldn't get any worse, they got worse.

Without asking my opinion, Howard had decided that Leon would live inside a kennel in the backyard. One of the first things I did at my "new house" was put Leon in the kennel. He would be outside and alone, like a bad dog sent to dog prison for his many shoe chomping and peeing-on-stuff crimes.

Setting Leon down, I whispered in his ear, "Heads up, buddy. We are not meant for this place. Hopefully, Mom will see that, too. But Howard has got her under some kind of spell. We'll give her a week, maybe less. Before this coming Sunday, we'll be busting out of here. When you hear me say the words *monkey butt*, get ready to run for daylight. That's when we'll make a break for it."

Leon farted. It's his way. And it meant he agreed with my plan.

I had just left the kennel when my dog jumped up and started barking. I looked at where Leon's eyes were aimed, across the yard, and saw nothing, no animals or people. Not even a lightning bug or a moth.

"What are you barking at, Leon?" I asked. "The shadows?"

He kept yipping. I looked closer and saw the strangest thing. There were footprints in the grass like someone was walking away from the kennel. But again, no one was there.

That was the first time I felt a strange taste in my mouth, metallic and mushy. Imagine eating a stack of ten Pringles potato chips flavored with fear—it tasted just like that. I stood there breathless, shaking, and watching footprints bending the grass, moving toward the wooden fence. Seconds later the gate creaked open, even though no one had opened it. The gate closed—on its own, it seemed—and an unseen hand pushed the latch into a slot, locking in Leon and me.

My body flew into full losing-it-mode. "Help-help-help me!" I screamed, before I could think about whether screaming was such a hot idea. Even though I was with Leon, I didn't feel safe. He's not exactly a guard dog. Leon could be easily bribed into silence with Milk-Bones, and not even the flavored ones that come in multiple colors. Nope, Leon was a sucker for the basic brown ones.

Mom and Howard and Mac and Tabitha came running from the front yard.

"What's wrong, Honey?" Mom said, throwing a protective arm around me.

12

I checked the fence and the grass. Nothing freaky was happening. Whatever was here, was gone now. Even Leon had stopped barking.

Howard and his kids and my mom stared at me, waiting for an explanation. What could I say? My proof had walked away. So, I just pointed like an idiot and stuttered. "I … I saw … well … I thought I saw a snake, but it was just a stick. Sorry for the false alarm." When I had to, I could lie pretty good.

Howard smiled.

"Poor thing, you're shivering. It's no wonder. A big move is never easy. By tomorrow morning you'll start to feel like yourself again, just watch." Reaching out, he patted my head again. That was twice now. He would pay.

Howard and his crew, including my mom, walked off. Watching them go, I wondered if the weird stuff had really happened.

"Think, Bertie. Figure it out."

Counting on my fingers, I replayed the last hour. The inexplicable evidence I'd seen and felt. I wanted it to make sense.

"One, I'm dead tired from the long drive.

"Two, my heart is shattered from leaving my father and my friends.

"Three, I'm seeing double from all the bizarro things that started after we passed the Altoona sign. The wolf thing, the

13

warning whisper thing, the metallic taste thing, the frozen chill of a *not-my-loneliness* feeling thing.

"Four, I don't believe a single word of what I'm saying.

"Five, this is real, Bertie! You totally had a close encounter with ... what? A ghost? An evil spirit? Or some kind of Hogwarts banshee, or a fallen angel, or a demonic phantom ..."

CRACK.

Behind me, a twig snapped.

Shrieking in horror, I spun around.

It wasn't a phantom or a banshee, it was Mac. His big eyes blinked up at me.

"Do you always talk to yourself?" he asked.

3

Strawberry Pop-Tarts

I wanted to go straight to bed and sleep for a week, but Howard insisted that "the entire family" gather at the kitchen table for a treat. For the first time I hated the word *family*. It was supposed to mean me and my parents and Leon, and no one else.

The snack was strawberry Pop-Tarts and almond milk. I don't despise almond milk, but I prefer real milk from real cows. I can't even guess how they get milk from a dry and bland nut. I'm guessing it's painful for the poor almonds.

Before we ate, Howard said grace. The Mortons were more devout than Mom and me. We attended church, just not religiously. I listened to Howard thanking God for Mom and me safely arriving in Altoona, and for all of us joining together as a family. Us, a family? No way! I was worried that

15

Howard would pressure me to go to church every Sunday morning. I'd probably have to wear a fancy dress and nice shoes, which I would hate, and be friendly to complete strangers for two hours, which would be impossible.

"What a great night!" Howard beamed. "The first of many, many great nights."

Tabitha rolled her eyes and moved the Pop-Tart from one side of her plate to the other. Mac gobbled his pastry quickly, then chugged his almond milk down in what seemed like one big gulp. He slammed his empty cup on the table and said, "Done," as if there was a prize to follow.

"One of the top five nights of my life," Mom said, squeezing Howard's hand and smiling. "A fresh start for all of us."

Everyone looked at me like they were expecting me to say something sweet or memorable or funny. Instead, I yawned like I was bored to death, which set off a round of yawns from Mom and Howard and Tabitha and Mac. It felt like a small victory.

"Hey, Bertie," Mac said. "Do you want to see my room when we are done here? I have some really cool stuff."

Before I could say a word, Tabitha answered for me.

"Your bedroom is not the major attraction you think it is," she told her brother. "I'm sure Bertie is tired and wants to crash."

That was actually true. I was running on fumes. And on anger, a potent fuel.

Halfway through the snack, I surveyed the table. Tabitha stared blankly ahead, and Mac smiled at me. I didn't smile back. I had a choice to make. I could either try to join the Mortons' parade of happiness, or I could bring them down to my level of gloom and doom. I went for door number two.

"Guys?" I pretended that an important thought had just occurred to me. "I totally forgot that a few days ago I read a blog that said eating sweets after ten PM is scientifically linked to insomnia, explosive diarrhea, and screaming nightmares."

Mac pushed his plate away, and his eyes widened with worry. I glanced at my mom, who was giving me a stern *not-another-word* glare.

"Don't let that newsflash freak you out," I said. "The medical profession is always flip-flopping their 'eat this, don't eat that' policy, right?" I bit my Pop-Tart, which was quite tasty. It washed away the metallic taste of evil I had in my mouth.

I almost felt better, until the kitchen lights went off and on and off and on, and then the TV in the living room turned itself on, and then off, and then on.

Gazing at me, Mac blurted, "It's okay, Bertie, it's not a ghost."

"A ghost?" Howard chuckled. "Oh no, we don't have ghosts, but we do have power surges along the entire block.

17

The electric company assured everyone it would be fixed soon. And we're doing some wiring upgrades on our own as well."

"Is it dangerous?" my mom asked.

Before Howard could respond, I chimed in.

"That depends on whether this place is haunted by a witch that was burned at the stake several centuries ago, or some stir-crazy sea captain who murdered his crew in cold blood. That would be big-time dangerous."

My mom tightened. "Bertie!"

Unable to stop talking, I finished the thought. "Or the ghost could be a desperately lonely but kindhearted orphan boy who died in a horrific sweatshop fire. On the danger scale, I'm thinking that would be a lot less."

Cutting me off, my mother rose from her chair. She tried so hard to appear calm, but her tone betrayed her. "How imaginative of you, young lady. Come with me."

Uh-oh, I must've taken things too far. Again.

In the hallway, Mom bent down so we were eye-to-eye. That was like getting a Grim Reaper tarot card. Basically, I was dead. We were out of earshot of the Mortons, but she spoke in a ferocious hush.

"Did we or did we not discuss the importance of first impressions?" she asked.

I needed to make her understand.

"Mom, something is wrong here. Something bad is going to happen."

She narrowed her eyes.

"Something bad has already happened. You've been a disaster on wheels since you stepped out of the car."

Reaching out, I put my hands on her arm. "Mom, I swear, there really is something haunted in this place, I can feel it. I'm trying to protect you!"

Her face tightened. "No, Bertie, I'm trying to protect *you*."

"So you feel it too?" I said, hopeful.

"You're not hearing me. I'm trying to protect you from you!" Mom said with a mix of love and disappointment that only the best mothers can master. "Can't you see what's really happening here, Bertie? You're feeding the wrong wolf."

My whole body clenched into a fist of shame.

Was I actually seeing things that go bump in the night, or was I trying to ruin my mother's happiness? Could I really be that mean and selfish? I stopped myself from answering that last question because I knew I totally could be that mean and selfish. I looked at my mom and swallowed. For a second, I was sure I hadn't seen anything spooky. Then, over Mom's shoulder, I watched the lights go on and off once again. In the flickering mix of dark and light, a ghostly figure swept across the kitchen.

"GHOST!" I shrieked.

4

Hiding Under a Sheet

My post-ghost encounter plan was to hide from my mom, the Mortons, my new life, and whoever that horrifying thing was that floated across the kitchen.

But I couldn't even do that.

Turns out, my room was a fire hazard. The electrician Howard had hired to replace the old wiring in my new bedroom wouldn't be finished for another week. So until then, I'd be bunking with Tabitha in her room. This was another disaster waiting to happen. I would be venturing into enemy territory.

Tabitha hadn't complained or made funny faces or anything like that, but we were the same age, and we both knew I was invading her space. "You can take the bed," she said when I stood in her doorway. She was lying on the floor on a pink sleeping bag, reading a graphic novel. "In a few days, we'll switch. Cool?"

I went to the bed. I didn't want to talk or explain myself. I just wanted to hide under the enemy's sheets and dream I was anywhere but here.

Tabitha had other plans. She spoke quietly, but firmly.

"Yesterday, I promised my dad that I'd make the best of this new … of our new situation. And I'm going to keep my promise. Because he's happy. Happier than I've seen him in like so long. Like forever. Do you understand what I'm saying?"

"Howard is happy?" I said, doubtful.

It wasn't the response Tabitha was looking for.

"Look, Bertie, I get that this is hard for you, I really do. It isn't easy for Mac and me, either." Tabitha looked away, trying to find the perfect words floating in the air. "What happened tonight, I can't tell if you were acting that way on purpose because you're mad or if you're just trying to be funny."

She was starting to tick me off.

"Hey, that wasn't acting! I saw something funky in the kitchen!"

Tabitha nodded. She was much calmer than me, which ticked me off even more.

"Then why didn't anyone else see it?" she asked. "My dad and Mac and I were in the kitchen. Shouldn't we have seen it, too? And why would a ghost just happen to show up on the night you arrive?"

"Hey, enough with the questions," I said. "I don't know what's going on, okay? It's not like I see weird things all the time."

"Okay, fine. What did the ghost look like?"

She wasn't going to let me off easy. And now I was fully ticked.

"I already told everybody, I couldn't see an actual face," I said. "It's hard to explain. It was like a white shadow or something … Know what? Let's forget the whole thing happened. I just want to sleep now."

Tabitha rolled her eyes. It seemed like she was judging me, which I *always* hated. "Do you pray before you go to sleep?" she asked.

"Pray?" I said. "No, not normally. But tonight I'm going to pray I wake up in my own bed in North Carolina, and all this Pennsylvania nonsense was a bad dream."

To my surprise, Tabitha laughed. "Hope that comes true for you."

To my surprise, I also laughed. It was a nice moment, actually. Then Tabitha asked, "So do you believe in God and heaven and stuff?"

Not a question I thought I'd be answering tonight. But I

22

could tell Tabitha was trying to understand me. And since I felt so misunderstood, I appreciated the effort.

"I believe in God, but I don't think He has time to hear our prayers every day," I said. "He's busy making billions of stars and planets, after all."

"Hmmm. Never thought about it like that," Tabitha said. "Well, I hope you don't mind if I pray before I conk out."

I figured she would pray silently, but I was wrong.

"Dear Lord," she said, after weaving her hands together and closing her eyes. "Thank you for this beautiful day, and for Bernice and her mom coming to live with us in our house, which has no ghost witches, ghost ship captains, or ghost burned orphans, but it does have plenty of old electrical wiring. Please protect all of us from harm as we go forth in your world. Please watch over my mother in heaven, and let her know that Dad and Mac and I miss her every day. Amen." She opened her eyes and said, "Goodnight, Bertie."

"Goodnight," I said, feeling bad for being mean to a girl who had lost her mother. I couldn't even imagine how painful that must be. Mom had told me that Howard's wife had died from some kind of awful disease, but I was so upset about the news bomb that we were moving to Altoona, it didn't stick or feel real. I did not know the Mortons. I certainly didn't care much about them.

23

But that night in Tabitha's bedroom, so far away from Carver City and almost everyone I knew and loved, it stuck. I was ten feet from a girl whose mom had died, and it was the same story with the boy down the hall, Mac. Even though my situation was awful, their situation was much worse.

Instead of telling Tabitha I was sorry, I buried myself under the sheet and tried to fall asleep. Part of me knew I should say something to Tabitha, but it would have to wait. I was far too busy worrying about escaping this dangerous place with my dog and my mother to worry about other people and their problems.

5

Scrambled Lives

I did not think I could possibly despise the Mortons more than I already did, until I discovered they were a bunch of early-risers and cheerful morning people. At about seven-thirty the next morning, Tabitha pushed my shoulder and woke me up. "It's time for breakfast. Since you guys showed up late, we let you sleep in."

Seven-thirty was sleeping in? On what horrible planet could that possibly be true?

I had gotten less than five hours of sleep. During the night I woke up, having to pee like crazy. Trudging into the Mortons' hallway, I heard someone, an eerily disembodied voice, calling my name in the darkness. "Bertie." Dashing inside Tabitha's room, I dove under the sheet and shivered for I don't know how long. I was so dead-tired that I eventually fell asleep.

I was the last to arrive at the breakfast table. Howard and my mom were sitting so close together, it looked like they were wearing one pair of pajamas. After throwing up a little bit in my mouth, I sat down, ready to shred the first person who looked at me.

Unfortunately, it was my mom. She seemed genuinely happy. Grossly happy. So happy she glowed, like the night before. How does a person glow in daylight? She was defying the laws of physics.

"Howard made your favorite breakfast, honey," Mom said. "Wasn't that nice of him?"

I eyed the plate of scrambled eggs, hash browns, and orange wedges in front of me. The meal looked tasty, I hated to admit. After Tabitha said grace, our first breakfast as a "family" was underway.

"Did you sleep well, Bernice?" Howard asked.

"No, I didn't," I said, cutting through his overly nice fake concern with my own brand of nasty.

Mom cleared her throat in my direction.

"Not to seem rude," I went on, "but I can't stand to be called Bernice. Please call me Bertie, okay?"

"Bertie it is." Howard smiled so wide I could've shoved a banana in his mouth sideways.

I smiled back.

"Thank you. And, not to seem ruder, Howard, but I'm like one hundred percent certain your house is haunted by an evil hoodoo spirit."

Ah, I said it. And if felt good. Everyone swapped quick looks. The glowing smile on my mother's face dimmed as she braced herself. *Here we go again!* It was obvious that neither my mom or any of the Mortons had believed a single word I'd said since I arrived. Everyone was just too nice to say they thought I was nuts or was being purposefully difficult. Howard even tried to redirect the topic.

"Oh, Bertie, I'm so sorry. I take it you had a nightmare?"

A nightmare? The nerve of this bonehead! Before I could tear apart Howard's nightmare theory, something happened. And it happened in a split second. Everything slowed down. And I heard a warm, beautiful voice in my head telling me to *stop talking, and start eating.*

There was something about the voice I liked. It was so different from the dark, lonely whisper that had terrified me the night before. This voice had a feeling or a vibe or whatever people call weird things they can't explain. My great-aunt Tillie—super fun lady, tarot card fanatic, and total nutjob—called them "woo-woo moments." Whatever it was, I suddenly didn't want to ruin breakfast for my mother. I wanted her to glow the way she was glowing before I told

Howard his beloved house was haunted by evil ghosts. So I stopped talking and started eating.

For that moment at least, I gave in. I surrendered.

I let Howard have his nightmare theory, and I let my mom have her glow. I felt a rush of goodness course through my body. It felt amazing. No joke. I felt happy and full of good intentions. I even made a silent vow that I would try to be kind to Howard, Tabitha, and Mac for the rest of the morning.

Vows can be tricky.

In my defense, Howard got overly mushy. His huge head nodded at me like he could read my deepest thoughts. "The first few nights in a new house can feel so awkward and uncomfortable, Bertie, but I hope in time you will feel more at home here, and that you will also think of us as your family."

Did he seriously just say that? Strike one.

I was one minute into the vow. My smile had vanished, but I was still silent.

Then Mac stepped up to the plate and took a swing. He pointed out to everyone that I had a gigantic sleep booger in my left eye. "It's all gooey and gross. Looks like you got brains oozing out of your eyeball."

Strike two.

Truth be told, two strikes are all you get with me.

"Thanks, Mac!" I said, reaching for a napkin. "I really appreciate how helpful and observant you are. By the way, the nightmare I had was actually about you. Turns out, you will never grow above four feet tall, and you will have chronic acne well into your adult years. Sorry, kid." I shoveled a forkful of eggs into my mouth. "You win some and you lose some."

Mac sniffled, piecing together his dire future. Then came a torrent of tears, and a huge snot bubble. I glanced at Mom. Definitely not glowing anymore. Howard looked somewhere between shocked and sad. Tabitha glared at me and scowled.

Playing innocent, I shrugged. "What? Howard wanted me to act like I'm part of the family."

My jerky smile quickly faded. Mac was still blubbering, blowing his nose into a napkin. I had ruined his breakfast. What was wrong with me? I wanted to crawl underneath the table, and hope there was a magic portal that would whoosh me back to Carver City, to my old life of just one day ago.

6

Ten Days to Escape

"Whoa, Peach Pie, let's back it up a meter or two," my father said over my cell phone.

We were Facetiming. I was standing in the Mortons' driveway, and he was inside a North Carolina airport, waiting to board a flight to Los Angeles. He looked so handsome. I missed him so much, I had to stop myself from collapsing.

"Let me see if I understand you clearly, Bertie." My father liked to summarize what people said. As I mentioned, he's a semi-famous attorney, and summarizing is his way of making you sound, well, unsound. My mom said he had turned it into an art form.

"Not one other person in the Morton house heard, or saw, or felt, any of the things you have heard, and seen, and felt," Dad said. "No ghosts or spirits or spectral beings?"

Swallowing a breath, I clutched his small image like it was a lifeline.

"Well, no, but I did," I said. "I really did. Something bad is happening here, Daddy, you got to believe me. Something bad is coming for me and mom and even Leon."

My father said nothing. He just looked at me.

Another lawyer trick. Stewing in the silence, you start to wonder if you should go ahead and plead insanity. Only I wasn't surrendering twice in one day. Dad was the only person in the world who totally understood me, and I needed him to understand me now. Finally, he spoke up. "So, what you are really telling me is that you are concerned about your mother's health and welfare?"

The odd phrasing threw me a bit, but I nodded, "Yes, Daddy, I am."

He gestured to a gate agent that he needed one more minute, then he looked into his cell and spoke quickly. "In that case, you need to cut out this nonsense, Bertie. I mean it. You need to try harder to get along with the Mortons and stop stirring up trouble for your mother. And, more importantly, for yourself. Be better than this."

"Daddy, I'm not lying."

He cut me off. It hit me that I had inherited this impolite trait from him.

31

"Well, you're sure not telling the truth. Forgive me for sounding harsh, Fluffy Stuff, but I've got to board this flight, so we are going to have to wrap this up. You know full well there is no such thing as ghosts. If you said something like that to me on the witness stand, I'd rip your testimony to pieces."

"I'm not a defendant, I'm your daughter," I said. "And I'm scared."

He cut me off again, this time sympathetically.

"Bertie, I'm sorry you're hurting. It makes me hurt, too. But we are still sticking to the plan: I'll be in Altoona in ten days. We will figure this out, okay? Just ten quick days."

Ten days sounded like a life sentence. Or a death sentence. Water rose in my eyes. "Promise, Daddy? I need you to say you promise."

"Have I ever let you down?"

"That's a question, not a promise," I said.

"I promise, I promise, I promise. How's that?"

The image on my cell jittered as he speed-walked down the tunnel to his airplane. Blowing me a goodbye kiss, he made me promise I would try my best to be my best.

"I promise, I promise, I promise," I said.

The call ended. His image went dark. Warm tears fell down my cheeks.

Ten days till I escape, I thought. Ten lousy days.

7

"Monkey Butt!"

I n a full sprint, I ran to Leon's kennel, shouting our code words, "Monkey butt!"

Leon was asleep, so I yelled louder, "MONKEY BUTT!" I honestly expected my dog to jump up and run with me as we made our practice escape. But Leon just looked at me, probably wondering why I was running around like a headless chicken.

"Lucky for you this was just a drill," I said. "When it's time to activate the escape plan, you better put some pep in your step, pal." Bending down, I petted Leon's head and scratched his back. Now I had his full attention. A good scratch could do that.

Leon is what I call a "reverse rescue dog." He rescued my family. Well, for a little while anyway. Three years ago, when my parents were close to splitting up, he showed up on our front porch one day, muddy and in need of a bath. It was like he had chosen us for his new family. We all fell in love with Leon, even my dad, who does not normally like dogs, even though Leon is kind of lazy and sleepy, and he farts like there's no tomorrow. For a few magnificent months, peace and happiness returned to our family and to our house.

I will tell you a secret I didn't tell Tabitha: I prayed a lot back then.

Every night I'd pray that Leon's magic would continue to keep my mom and dad together. But the magic faded. My parents went back to arguing about every little thing. Eventually, they got divorced. There's only so much a dog can do for a family, I guess.

Looking down at Leon, I realized I had to do more to protect him, myself, and my mom. Something bad was coming our way. I could feel it in my bones.

So I thought of a new plan. A terrible and messy and wonderful plan to get us all back to North Carolina. My plan was to break up Mom and Howard before their wedding.

A curious voice pushed me out of my devious thoughts.

"Why is your dog so shy?"

Looking over my shoulder, I saw Mac approaching.

"You shouldn't sneak up on people," I said, giving Mac a royal stink-eye.

"I wasn't sneaking, I was walking."

I shrugged, *whatever*.

"Do you think I can pet him?" he asked.

"No," I said. "Leon does not like to be touched by strangers."

Mac wiggled his mouth like he was figuring out his next move. "I used to have a dog named Cosmo, but he ran away."

"That stinks," I said, softening. "Why did he run away?" I felt bad for the kid. It's tough when you lose a pet. At my house in Carver City, my backyard was pretty much a graveyard for lost pets, dead birds and bugs, and a roadkill skunk I had found.

"He was chasing a rabbit," Mac said. "They ran into the woods, and Cosmo got lost. But I think he's gonna come home soon. Cosmo and I were best friends. He's probably been searching for me while I've been looking for him."

"How long has he been gone?"

"Almost two years."

"Wow, long time," I said, trying not to make a face. "Especially in dog years."

"Cosmo loves me," Mac said. "He just got lost, is all. He could still come back."

There was no way Mac's dog would be coming home: two years was way too long. Cosmo was with another family, or dead, or running wild. But that's not what I told Mac.

"Never know," I said. "Miracles happen every day." Which was a lie. Miracles were as rare as rainbow zebras. Or attorney fathers canceling their business trips to Los Angeles to rescue their terrified daughters.

"Can I pet Leon just once?" Mac asked.

"Okay," I said, despising my weakness.

Mac came closer.

"Good doggy," he said, rubbing Leon's head and ears. Leon gave us looks I interpreted this way: *you guys don't have anything better to do?*

"Mac?" I said. "Leon has suffered enough excitement for one morning, so we should probably leave him alone for a while."

"I think your dog will become less shy when more time passes," Mac said, while I latched the kennel door. "Everyone is nervous when they meet new people. But it usually wears off."

Secretly, I thought Mac was smart for his age. Well, except for his dream about Cosmo coming home soon. Rather than correct Mac, I walked away, disliking myself for being such a big jerk.

In my head I heard the same six words thumping over and over, *Something horrible is going to happen,* like a demented disc jockey was playing a loop to torture me.

8

The Axeman

On my tenth birthday, my great-aunt Tillie, the same great-aunt my parents often pretended didn't exist, did a tarot card reading for me. Flipping cards on the table, she explained the difference between heaven and hell. "In heaven, everyone is doing stuff they want to do, Bertie. And in hell they are doing the *exact* same thing, only they don't want to do it."

At the time, it didn't make sense to me. But now I got it. I didn't want to be here. The Mortons' house was my personal hell.

To most people, it wouldn't look like it. The house was at the end of a road called Hickory Street, in an upper-class neighborhood. Everyone kept telling me the same thing over and over. "The neighborhood is so great, Bertie. You're going to love it."

To prove their point, Mac and Tabitha took me on a tour after lunch. "Bonding time," Howard called it. We hopped on our bikes and pedaled past big, clean houses. The yards were nice and green. Kids were at play, or dads or moms were mowing or gardening. Tall shade trees lined both sides of the street. Beams of sunlight poked through the thick branches like hundreds of little spotlights.

The Morton kids were practically tripping over themselves to be nice to me. It felt phony. When I mentioned I needed to be on the lookout for bees because I'm highly allergic and one sting would blow me up like a hot air balloon, I glimpsed a grinning Tabitha. It was like I could read the sinister thoughts churning in her mind. *Let's buy a honey-coated jumpsuit for Bertie!*

Our bike ride should've been peaceful, but I had an ominous feeling in my gut that it was all a setup. Actually, it felt like I was pedaling through a horror movie. Three kids ride down a lovely street, when … WHAM! Evil beasts pounce from the shadows and tear their bodies limb from limb.

"Look, Bertie. Pretty isn't it?" Tabitha pointed ahead as we turned a corner. As we got farther from Howard's house, a mountain just outside the town came into view. In the bright sunlight it looked blue and green and wise, like mountains sometimes do. It reminded me of home.

Brush Mountain, Mac said they called it. I gave it a jerky compliment. "It's dinky compared to the Great Smoky Mountains in North Carolina. More like an ambitious hill than an actual mountain."

Tabitha and Mac shared a frustrated glance. Our bonding wasn't going as planned. I told myself that I'd rather bond with a hungry grizzly bear, or a slithering rattlesnake, or bloodsucking leeches.

"Guys, let's be honest," I said. "The only reason we are doing this lame tour is because your dad made you do it."

"No he didn't," Tabitha said. "We're just trying to give you a chance."

"Why? I don't need any chances," I said. "I won't be staying in Altoona very long."

"Promise?" she said.

"Tabitha!" Mac scolded. "Dad said we gotta be nice to Bertie, no matter what. Plus, she let me pet Leon."

"Ah-ha!" I said, glaring at Tabitha. "Now who's the liar?"

Tabitha didn't like that one bit. Skidding her bike to a stop, she looked at me. "I'm not a liar! And I'm not some weirdo seeing things that aren't there."

Mac spoke up again. "Definitely not being nice."

I opened my mouth to say something mean, until I heard a loud *caw-caw-caw.* The noise drew my eyes to a crow in an oak tree. The bird stared at me like it knew me. Like it wanted to get my attention. *Caw-caw-caw!* I stuck my tongue out at the crow, then watched it fly away.

My eyes shot wide. I would've sworn the black crow had morphed into a dove or some kind of white bird. It was beautiful and creepy at once.

Maybe Tabitha was right. I was a weirdo who saw things that weren't there.

"Hey!" a man shouted. "You trying to get yourselves killed?"

The shout was so jarring, I nearly fell off my bike. Beside me, Tabitha's and Mac's jaws dropped. Under the oak tree stood a gigantic bearded man staring at us through a chain-link fence on his property. A six-foot-six beast of a man, clutching an axe. His hair, face, and clothes were filthy. The yard behind him was even worse. Junk everywhere. A broken-down truck that looked like it hadn't been driven in years, and was being slowly swallowed up by nature. A rusted washing machine and a stove with no door took up space where a sidewalk should've been. The fence surrounding his property was crowned with barbed wire, like Axeman was protecting treasure instead of junk. Suddenly, as if clouds were covering the sun, everything got darker. *Spooky* dark.

"Thieving kids scoping out my house. You're lookin' to

steal something, ain'tcha?" Axeman said with a smirk. He opened the squeaky gate. "Go on and try it, I dare you. Take one step inside my fence, and I got the legal right to cut you down to size."

Swinging the axe at the gnarled oak tree, the axeman sunk the blade into the trunk. THUNK! "Consider yourself warned. Y'all will feel my steel!"

"Move! Let's get out of here," Tabitha yelled to Mac and me.

Pedaling away as if our lives depended upon it, I said to Tabitha and Mac, "Shouldn't we call the cops? That dude totally wanted to kill us!"

"Nothing will happen if the police show up," Tabitha said. "My dad said even the cops are afraid of that guy. He's been scaring kids for years. We should've gone the other way."

Glancing back, I saw the axeman eyeballing us. A terrifying thought burst into my mind. Could he be the horrible thing that was going to happen?

Before taking the neighborhood tour, I'd made a mental list of all the awful, freaky, heartbreaking, rotten, scary things that had happened in Altoona. My *Reasons Why Mom and Leon and Me Must Escape Altoona Immediately* list.

As we raced away from the axeman, I added an item to that list. *A psychotic murderer lives down the street.*

9

Every Fool Needs a Quest

We had pedaled far enough that I couldn't see the axeman anymore. I was about to suggest that we take a different route home, when Mac veered off the street, toward a woods. Ditching his bike, he trotted down a trail like a little man on a mission.

"What's Mac doing?" I asked Tabitha, who didn't seem at all surprised by her brother's detour. She braked her bike and motioned to the woods.

"That's where Cosmo disappeared," she said. "We come here a few times a week, looking for him. Mac just doesn't get it. He's never going to find his dog in there. But good luck anyway."

Though Tabitha was right about Cosmo, a part of me admired Mac for not giving up on his lost dog. I dropped my bike and yelled to Mac, "Hey, wait up. I'll help you look for Cosmo."

"Really?" Mac turned. "Are you making fun of me?"

"Why would I make fun of you? Your dog's missing, and I want to help you find him," I said, feeling bad because I knew we had zero chance of actually finding Cosmo.

Mac shrugged. "Everyone always says it's hopeless."

Hurrying after him, I said, "Nothing is ever completely hopeless." My latest happy lie.

That was when Mac Morton surprised me with a hug. His thin arms clutched around me. I could feel his kindness. It was strange, but a good strange. I patted Mac on his shoulder and pushed him away, though not roughly.

"Look, you don't have to pretend to be nice to me, especially when your dad isn't around," I told him. "I'm not looking for a shiny new family, understand? The one I got is already messed up enough."

Mac offered no reaction whatsoever. He just said, "Can I tell you a secret?" I nodded that he could. "Tabitha's right, Bertie. You're weird."

"Well, that's not exactly a secret," I said.

Standing on his tippy-toes, Mac whispered in my ear. "The secret is … I like weird." His mischievous grin caught me off guard.

In North Carolina, I used to dream of having brothers and sisters to play with and pester, but that just wasn't in the tarot cards for me. I watched Mac move on, shouting into the dense woods, "Cosmo! Here, Cosmo!" For one quick flash I could envision Mac being my actual little brother, not just an annoying twerp I had to deal with until I escaped the Altoona horror-fest. We were kindred spirits, Mac and I. We loved dogs and weird stuff.

Branching off the trail beside Mac, I yelled, "Cosmo, are you here?" No response, of course. Cosmo was history. And even though Mac probably knew this better than anyone, he refused to give up on his missing dog. All at once, it hit me how much Mac and I shared. I still hadn't given up on my parents getting back together one day in the future.

Every fool needs something impossible to believe in, I guess.

10

Counting the Days

By now, eight X's were on my *Return to North Carolina* calendar. Eight days had passed since the video chat with my father, when he had promised to come and save Leon and me in ten days. Two days were left.

During that time, several things had happened. Routines formed. Each weekday, my mom and Howard worked at his optometrist office, which was attached to the house. Mom did his accounting and billing. During business hours, patients were always parking in the driveway. I'd hear a car pulling in, and I allowed myself to hope that my dad had come a few days early to fetch Leon and Mom and me. Each time it was someone else, a total stranger, and another punch to my gut.

A kid can only take so many punches.

Howard's electrician had finished rewiring my bedroom.

During dinner one night, Tabitha told me I could continue to sleep in her room if I was too frightened to sleep on my own. "You know, because of the hundreds of ghosts haunting our house."

Nice play, Shakespeare, I thought.

No way was I giving Tabitha gloating rights. Plus, when my dad showed up, I wanted him to know that I'd kept my promise to do my best. So I brave-faced it for Mom and the Mortons, and went up to my bedroom. "Sweet dreams, everybody," I said.

That first night I was so petrified, I didn't sleep more than a wink or two. Every time I heard a creaking sound somewhere in the house, or water rushing through pipes, I was certain ghosts were to blame. They were coming for me, getting closer.

During those days, perhaps the most spooky thing of all that happened was that nothing else spooky had happened. At least nothing spooky that I couldn't blame on my worried mind, picturing ghosts in every corner of the house, in the closets and in the cabinets. No homicidal spirits. No desperate whispers. No disembodied footprints. Not even a freaky light show flickering on and off. Nothing.

Had I imagined it all? I couldn't have.

On the ninth day, my fears were confirmed when

something horrible happened. I was feeding Leon dog chow in his kennel when I heard my dad's ringtone. The world brightened. "Hi, Daddy," I answered.

"No, Bertie, this is Mrs. Ida." Mrs. Ida was my father's secretary. She had elaborate hair, a syrupy accent, and said "real-real" a lot. "Bertie, I'm real-real sorry, honeybunch, but your daddy just found out he has to remain in Los Angeles longer than expected."

"What? He's not coming to Pennsylvania tomorrow?"

"Afraid not. He's real-real upset about it."

My heart jumped into my throat. I could barely speak. "No! He promised me, Mrs. Ida. He triple-promised. I need to speak to him. It's urgent."

"He's in court. Listen, Bertie, the case he's litigating turned upside down on him, and he's trying real-real hard to save the ship from sinking."

I hated myself for breaking down on the phone to Mrs. Ida, but there was no fighting it. Tears fell as I burst into stuttering sobs. "Yeah, well, my ship is sinking too, Mrs. Ida. And I-I-I've been doing my best to do my best!"

"Of that, I have no doubt. I'll give your daddy that message ASAP. He'll call you just as soon as he's able, okay? Hang in there, honeybunch." Mrs. Ida said she was real-real sorry twice more, and the signal went dead.

A part of me died with it. At that moment, I had never felt more lost or alone. Even with Leon there, eating his chow. I wanted to smash my phone, and Mrs. Ida, and even my father. It would serve him right if an evil ghost scared me to death, or the creepy man down the street chopped me to pieces with his axe. At my funeral, my dad would shout, "If only I'd kept my promise to Bertie! My triple-promise!" He'd throw himself onto my casket, or something dramatic and wickedly watchable that would get twenty gazillion hits on YouTube.

Sleeving tears from my cheeks, I heard laughter. Then I spotted Mac and Tabitha in the front yard, happy as could be. My mood darkened even more.

"Hey! That's my soccer ball" I yelled.

And that's how it began. Five angry words I will never be able to take back.

11

The Pink Soccer Ball

More laughter. Tabitha and Mac were kicking my pink soccer ball to each other. I shouted louder. "That's my soccer ball!" A picture of calm, they watched me as I stalked closer. I was looking for a fight, but they weren't cooperating.

"No it isn't, Bertie," Mac said.

"That *is* my ball. I brought it with me from North Carolina." I remembered squeezing the soccer ball between boxes of junk inside the trailer.

They stopped kicking the ball.

"Even if it is your ball, which it isn't," Tabitha said, "why can't we kick it? That's why soccer balls exist, so they can be kicked."

"You know what? You're right," I said, putting on a fake smile. "If you guys want to keep playing with *my* soccer ball, go right ahead. But first you got to go fetch it."

I booted the ball. It landed on the road and bounced across the street. Stopped rolling about fifteen feet onto someone's lawn.

"I'll get it," Mac said.

The first thing that happened was I saw and heard a crow up in a tree. That same bizarro crow I'd seen earlier, I was pretty sure. It shrieked at me. *Caw! Caw! Caw!*

All at once the world slowed down. Mac dashed after the ball and into the street. He didn't check for traffic. I heard my heartbeat, loud in my ears.

Ba-bump … Ba-bump … Ba-bump …

A silver pickup truck rounded a corner. The driver, a middle-aged man with curly brown hair, glanced down at a phone he held.

Ba-bump … Ba-BUMP … BA-BUMP …

Tabitha screamed, "Mac! Truck! Look out!"

My heart roared *BA-BUMP … BA-BUMP … BA-BUMP …*

Mac froze in the middle of the road as the truck got closer, speeding on through.

BA-BUMP-BA-BUMP-BA-BUMP …

"No!" I yelled.

BA-BUMP-BA-BUMP-BA-BUMP …

The crow shrieked, *CAW! CAW! CAW!*

The driver's eyes shocked wide.

BA-BUMP-BA-BUMP-BA-BUMP …

Tires bit the road as the driver tried to stop.

BA-BUMP-BA-BUMP-BA-BUMP …

The truck was about to hit Mac, brakes squealing from the pressure.

CAW! CAW! CAW!

CRASH! SMACK! CRUNCH!

BA-BUMP-BA-BUMP-BA-BUMP!!!

The truck's front fender struck Mac and knocked him backward onto the road. When the truck stopped moving, Mac was underneath it.

Tabitha screamed in a way I had never heard before, as she ran to her brother. The kind of scream you'd never forget.

The driver jumped out of his truck and looked beneath it.

"Kid? Can you hear me? Help is on the way! Are you alive? Say something if you can hear me."

Mac said nothing. He wasn't moving, not at all.

The air thickened around me. I could not breathe. I was going under. Mac had run across the street because of something stupid I did. And now he was lying on the road, under a truck. Was this really happening? I was pretty sure I had killed the kid.

The door to Howard's office flew open. Mom and Howard, wearing crisp white clothing, burst out of the office and ran to the accident scene.

"Mac! Oh my God! Oh my God!" Howard cried out. He dove to the street so he could get a clear view of his son under the pickup. "Mac, say something. Tell me you're okay, Mac! Please tell me you're okay." Reaching for Mac's left arm, Howard took Mac's pulse at the wrist. There was blood on Howard's coat sleeve. He said over and over, "Hang in there, Buddy. The ambulance is coming!"

Patients from Howard's office poured out into the street. Neighbors left their houses. Two older boys stopped their bikes. Drivers parked their cars, gawking at the little boy pinned under the pickup truck. Some people whispered prayers; others gasped and put their hands to their mouths and hearts.

A few minutes ago, the world had slowed. But now it sped up. Faster and faster like it was about to spin out of orbit. When my mom looked at me, my legs wobbled. A siren sounded in the distance. My heart was *this* close to erupting out of my chest. What had I done to the bighearted eight-year-old boy who loved dogs and weirdness, and who wasn't afraid to invest in lost causes?

Lights flashed as the ambulance arrived. Two medics

52

jumped out. Howard scrambled out of the way as the medics slid under the truck. Working together, they fitted Mac with a neck brace and readied a backboard, which I recognized from watching Carolina Panthers football games with my dad. They used them on players whenever they suspected serious neck or back injuries.

A growing crowd of bystanders watched the medics work. I shivered. Even the filthy axeman was there, recording the events on his old cell phone, like an innocent boy getting struck by a truck was entertaining. The medics slid Mac onto the backboard and into their ambulance. Howard tried to crawl inside, but one of the medics told him to follow the ambulance in his car. A door slammed shut. Away they went, siren blaring.

Howard and Tabitha hurried to Howard's minivan. Through the blurry haze of my falling tears, I caught Howard's gaze. Face red and blotchy, Howard waved me away, loud and sharp. "Ride with your mother, Bertie!"

My mom was waiting for me in the driver's seat. Climbing inside, I buckled up, numb and afraid. Mom backed up our car onto the road. We drove in silence for about a minute. She put her hand on my shaky knee. Looking up at her, I wanted to confess my sins. I wanted my mom to forgive me, and then lecture me about kindness, and putting other people first. I wanted to feel like I was her not-so-terrible daughter.

But all I could say was, "Mom, they're going to blame me." My head hung low. "I don't know if I should go to the hospital. I don't know if they will even want me there."

"No one will blame you," she said.

"No, they will! Tabitha will definitely blame me!"

"Bertie, you need to calm down. This is not about you, understand?"

"But don't you want to know about—"

"We will talk later about everything," she said. "Right now, we need to find out Mac's condition at the hospital. Then we can figure out what's what. Got it?"

There was no anger in her voice. She gave me a look of love. A mother's love. It wounded me even deeper. Mac Morton and I would now be forever entwined, tangled up. I would always be the girl who caused Mac to be hit by a truck. He was badly hurt, and it was my fault. Depending on what happened next, lives hung in the balance. If Mac died, in a way, I would too. And that would mean the end of my mother.

Straining against my seatbelt, I clutched my knees to my chest. Like *Alice in Wonderland*, I wanted to shrink down so small I could crawl inside the glove box and hide. The shame of what I had done cut so deep, I didn't want anyone to see me, especially my mom. When she found out that I was the reason Mac was riding in an ambulance, she would never look at me the same way again.

Mom turned onto the road for St. Anne Hospital, and my stomach clenched. Dark thoughts bounced around my brain like a bullet ricochet. Since we'd arrived in Altoona, I had been warning my mom and my dad and the Mortons that something horrible was going to happen.

And now I finally realized the harsh truth. *I was the something horrible.*

12

"Do Something, Bertie!"

Tabitha and Howard were in the emergency room waiting area when Mom and I showed up. Tabitha was crying. Taking Howard's hands, Mom said, "What do we know?"

Looking dazed and desperate, Howard said, "Mac's in a coma. The doctors rushed him straight to the operating room." His voice was breaking. "They said he has internal bleeding, a punctured lung, and other injuries."

They hugged. Howard sobbed. A nurse piloted the four of us to a bank of elevators. Riding up to the fifth floor, Tabitha shot me an evil look, so I kept my gaze locked on the floor numbers. If there had been an escape hatch in that elevator, I would've taken it. My future stepsister wanted to throw me off the hospital roof. I didn't blame her.

The car opened to a big sign that read *Surgical Intensive*

Care Unit. Howard signed in at the nursing desk. The rest of us claimed nearby chairs. I sat by myself, pretty sure that my face was a billboard for guilt and regret. Did everyone know what I had done to Mac by stupidly kicking the ball across the street? It sure felt like it. I had done rotten things before, but this was rottenness on a whole other level. Dark and distressing possibilities struck me like a karate kick to the teeth, one after the other. WHACK! What if Mac was paralyzed? WHACK! Or brain-damaged? WHACK! Or put on life support? WHACK! Or, the harshest kick of all, he died? WHACK!

Even if Mac completely healed and woke up, I would still be "that" girl. Stained and rotten forever. Nothing after today would ever be the same. If my great-aunt Tillie gave me another tarot card reading, every card she flipped would be Death.

Mac was in surgery for five hours. Tabitha didn't look at me once that entire time. She was pretending I didn't exist.

A surgeon in blue scrubs, Dr. Myles Carson, came to talk to us. He said that the surgeries had gone well, but Mac had a "long and difficult road ahead." First, Mac needed to wake up from his coma—he was not sure when that would happen— and then they'd worry about things like physical therapy when his broken bones healed: a broken leg, a broken arm, a broken hipbone, and four broken ribs. But Dr. Myles was far more worried about the injury to Mac's brain than anything else. It was life-threatening, he said.

"The swelling in Mac's brain is restricting blood flow," Dr. Myles said. "If his brain doesn't get enough blood, there could be permanent damage." He looked at Tabitha and at me before continuing in a hushed tone. "I drilled a small hole into Mac's skull to drain excessive cerebrospinal fluid through a shunt and a catheter."

Each new detail made me sicker with worry. I wanted to curl up and die like how spiders die. Become a shriveled papery thing that could be blown across the room with a gentle puff of air.

"Does Mac have a chance of making a full recovery?" Howard asked the doctor.

Dr. Myles gave Howard a sympathetic nod, and put a hand on his shoulder. "Anything is possible, Mr. Morton. But at this point the odds are not good, I'm afraid. These next few days will be critical. Let's try to remain positive."

Howard and my mom gave each other a horrified look. Howard rubbed the creases on his forehead and sighed. Mom grabbed his hand. Directly behind them was a soda machine. My eyes narrowed. The LED readout blinked, and then a bizarre message scrolled. *Do something, Bertie! Do it now!*

I looked around, wondering if anyone else had seen the flashing words. No one had. What did it mean? What could I do?

Dr. Myles was about to leave when an ice-cold shiver shot through my bones. Quick as a cobra, I grabbed the surgeon's arm. And these words popped out of my mouth, loud and direct. "Don't tell us you're afraid, Dr. Myles. Tell us you will find a way to heal Mac, understand? You *will* save Mac's life!"

Howard, my mom, two nurses, and nearly everyone else in that part of the ward stared at Dr. Myles and me. Dr. Myles' jaw dropped, and he slipped a pen into a coat pocket. "I will do everything I possibly can to save your brother, young lady."

He broke free and marched away. Howard gazed at me in a new way. "Thanks for that, Bertie. Those words needed to be said."

I don't know what made Tabitha angrier, that the doctor thought I was related to Mac, or that her father was being nice to me. Now, she stopped pretending I wasn't there. Shaking her head, she blurted. "No, no! No Dad, don't thank her." Tabitha pointed a finger at me. "She's the one who kicked the soccer ball across the street! This is *all Bertie's fault!*"

13

Lies

"Yes, I kicked the ball," I said, feeling a surge of anger. "But it's *not* my fault. Mac chased after the ball on his own. I didn't tell him to do that."

"Liar!" Tabitha said. "You kicked the ball and said, 'go fetch it.'"

"That's not how it happened!" I said.

"Have you told the truth since you got here?" Tabitha said. "Own up to what you did and what you said, Bertie. Be a good person for *once* in your life!"

Panic shot through me.

"I did not tell Mac to chase after the ball," I lied. "And besides, everyone knows to look both ways before crossing the street."

Clenching fists, Tabitha stepped toward me, but Howard slid between us. My mom was shocked into silence.

60

"Enough! Calm down, girls," Howard said, looking at Tabitha, and then at me. "This isn't the time or place."

My stomach gurgled. A thick black fear bubbled up around me like one of those prehistoric tar pits that sunk dinosaurs. For the fiftieth time in the last six hours, I sleeved away tears. "None of this is my fault," I repeated, even if I didn't really believe it myself.

"Bertie, not another word," my mom said, her face showing anger.

"Nobody believes you, anyway," Tabitha added. "It should've been *you* who got hit by that truck, not Mac!"

"Tabitha Morton!" Howard said, knitting together his eyebrows. "Apologize to Bertie. You will apologize this second, hear me?"

It was pretty sure it was the first time Howard had remembered to call me "Bertie" and not "Bernice," but I couldn't be happy about it.

Looking up at her father, Tabitha gave him a simple and defiant "No." Then she pointed down the hallway. "Look, it's Mac. They're bringing him out of surgery, Dad."

We all turned. Orderlies were wheeling Mac to his room. Without speaking, we all moved closer to Mac. His face was ghostly white, marked with cuts and bruises. Eyes shut from the coma. Bandages were wrapped around his head like a turban.

His right arm and leg were locked in casts. An oxygen tube pumped air into his nostrils, and monitors blinked and beeped all kinds of readings and measurements that only doctors and nurses understood. He looked so… so little and so hurt.

Howard and Tabitha hurried alongside the orderlies as a nurse opened the door to Mac's room. Taking Mac's left hand, Howard spoke to him. "Hi, Mac, it's Dad. Tabitha and I are here for you," he said, his voice trembling. "Bertie and her mother are here, too. Your family is here, Mac." He mopped sweat from his forehead with a Kleenex and sighed. "If you can hear me, Mac, this is what we need you to do. We need you to believe that you can be well again. Will you do that for us, buddy? Will you? Because we believe it. We believe it so much."

Gut-wrenching. Mac, Howard, and Tabitha and even my mom were paying the price for my stupidity. How could I have let him run into the street? I rubbed more tears from my eyes.

"We need to give them some time alone, Bertie," my mom spoke in a hush, eyeing me suspiciously.

It seemed like she wanted to give me a hug, but she wouldn't allow herself to do that. Instead she gave me a twenty-dollar bill. Did she see me differently? Placing her hand on my shoulder like a football coach, she said, "Go get some air and something to eat. And if you can, say a prayer for Mac."

"I've said a hundred prayers already," I mumbled. "But I'll say a hundred more if it will help. A thousand more."

Mom was reading me. My trembling fingers. My damp eyes. My jagged breath. She must've known that Tabitha was right, that I had done something unforgivable. "I'll text you when it's okay to come up," she said.

Do you ever get that *no one in the world wants to be near me* feeling? That's what I had. Only it wasn't just a feeling, it was a fact.

I stepped into an empty elevator. I pressed the "one" button. The "two" button lit up. I pressed "one" again. The "two" button lit up even brighter.

Down I went. My phone pinged with a text.

You need to start paying attention, Bernice.

I gaped at the screen. The Caller ID read "From The Unknown."

Ping

Another text.

Get off at the 2nd floor.

Ping.

The final text.

Time 2 begin, Bernice.

My eyes widened. Begin what, exactly?

14

Light Storm

For a few moments I stood in a second floor hallway like an idiot, gaping at my phone screen and the mysterious texts.

Why did this stuff keep happening to me? My great-aunt Tillie once told me that tons of people have some serious hefty karmic debts to pay off. "But you don't have to worry about that, B," she said. "Your soul is as clean as any I've ever seen."

Hate to break it to you, Tillie, but I ain't that clean.

I smelled lavender. Looking up, a tall woman wearing glamorous sunglasses walked past me. She was strikingly pretty, and she looked sort of familiar. A wave of déjà vu hit me. I was ninety percent certain I had I seen this woman back home in Carver City.

She continued down the hall, then she opened a room door and went inside.

Before I knew it, I was standing at the same door. It didn't lead to a patient's room; it was the entrance to the hospital's chapel. Above the door I read a painted quote: *We are not human beings having a spiritual experience. We are spiritual beings having a human experience.* It was from some dead French guy named Teilhard de Chardin.

Opening the heavy wooden door, I stepped inside the chapel. Symbols for various religions hung on the walls. Seated in a mahogany chair, I saw the woman praying beside an altar filled with flickering candles. Taking a seat behind her, I said a prayer of my own for Mac.

Finishing my prayer in silence, I opened my eyes. The woman was gone. Where could she have gone to that quickly and quietly? She had left her sunglasses by the candles. Grabbing the glasses, I hurriedly pushed through the chapel door. "Ma'am, you forgot your…"

But the long hallway was empty. How could that be?

I went inside the chapel, just as beams of sunlight struck the stained glass window. The brilliant colored light blinded me. I shut my eyes, but I could see intense reds, oranges, yellows, blues, and greens swirling behind my lids.

"Hello," a female voice whispered. "Do you need instructions or something? What do you think the sunglasses are for? Put 'em on, professor, let's go!"

Blinded by the light, I followed her instructions. I put on the sunglasses and opened my eyes.

"Whoa!" The room had changed.

Everything glowed as if it was alive and breathing. Even the sunlight was breathing.

The candles spouted flames two feet high.

The chairs and benches had turned into living trees, their branches growing sideways.

The carpet on the floor was a crystal blue lake I could dive into.

"Get ready, girlfriend," the voice said. "I'm about to blow your mind!"

15

A More Better Bertie

A girl who looked exactly like me stood with hands on her hips. She was even wearing the same clothes.

"Ack!" I was so shocked by the sight I tripped and fell— off went the sunglasses. I looked around the chapel, but the other me had vanished. The blue carpet was no longer a lake.

With shaky hands, I picked up the glasses and inspected them. They must have had trick lenses, because when I put them on, everything was back to normal. I looked to my right and then behind me. No twin. No flames. No living trees.

"Yoo-hoo, sweet cheeks, over *here*."

I glanced to my left. The other me sat on a bench, crossing her eyes and puckering her lips. I couldn't help but laugh, even though I was freaked out by the sight of a second me.

When I'm nervous expect laughter or even girlish giggles. It's humiliating.

"Now that I have your attention, please leave the glasses on so we can have a Bertie-to-Bertie chat," she said.

I didn't listen. Instead, I yanked the glasses off like they were possessed by demons. The other me was gone. Was I losing my mind? Was I destined to be the new great-aunt Tillie? Mental illness ran in my family. Now it was my turn to show symptoms.

Curiosity got the better of me. I slid the glasses on. My twin stood before me, nose-to-nose. I gasped.

"Relax, Bertie. You're not the new Tillie," she said. "You're you, and you've got to wise up, girl. And I mean fast. You've been making some major league idiotic decisions."

I tore off the glasses, and the other Bertie was gone. The room fell silent, except for my head pounding like a war drum.

This could not be happening. Since the first night I drove past that cursed *Welcome to Altoona* sign, nothing had gone the way it should have: I'd cracked. Wolves in the road, footsteps in the grass, ghosts in the house, the axeman, the strange crow, Mac getting hit by a truck, LED messages from the snack machine, weird texts from no one, and now I'm talking to another me? No, it was too much. The trauma of watching Mac suffer had pushed my brain past the brink.

Looking down at the sunglasses in my hand, I swallowed a long breath. Despite my fragile mental condition, I put them on. The other me stood to my left.

"Who are you?" I asked.

"Dude, you already know who I am," she said. "I'm you. Not to seem judgy, but I'm a better version of you. And because I'm better, and smarter, and kinder, I see life differently, like how it's supposed to be."

"Better Bertie?" I huffed. "Well, lucky for me you didn't get judgy." Looking closer, I saw she had a glow around her. It looked amazing. But no way was I telling her.

"Imagine a horse race with two horses," Better Bertie said. "One horse…"

"Could they be wolves instead of horses?" I asked.

"What?"

"Wolves! No horses!"

"Okay. If you want wolves, fine."

"I want wolves."

"So one wolf takes the high road, and one wolf takes the low road. It's up to you which wolf you want to ride. Not that anyone actually rides wolves." Better Bertie seemed a bit flustered. "Look, the visual works *way* better with horses."

"Relax, I get the gist," I said. "There are two of us, a

higher me and a lower me. But if that's true, why am I just meeting you now?"

"You're not. You've always known about me. And you always forget me," Better Bertie said. "Remember on your sixth birthday when you saw a meteor shower and you felt so incredibly lucky to be alive? Or the day Leon appeared on our porch and your heart swelled fifty times bigger because you knew you had just found a new best friend?"

"So wait, you're only here for the happy times?"

"Baby girl, I *am* the happy times," Better Bertie said.

"What's that supposed to mean?"

"It means I am you when you choose to be happy."

"Oh, c'mon. You don't get to choose to be happy," I said.

"Sure you do," she said. "It doesn't feel like that because you keep choosing to be unhappy. Or choosing to be mean. Or angry. Or vengeful. Or difficult. Or dishonest."

"None of those were a choice!" I said. "They just were!"

Better Bertie shook her head.

"Sorry, Bertie, wrong answer. The correct answer is that every one of them was a choice." She grinned, and then she did a surprisingly good karate kick. "And when you choose love, or happiness, or gratitude, that's me. Ta-da!"

"If that's really true, then why would anyone choose to be unhappy?"

"Great question." Better Bertie smiled, but she didn't say anything.

"Well, are you going to tell me or not?"

"I have told you! Over the years, I've told you a million times. But since Mom and Dad's divorce, you've gotten too proud to listen. You would rather be *right* than happy. Nobody wins that way. This week alone you've made forty-seven terrible choices."

"Forty-seven?" I said. "Wow. Figured there'd be more."

"Oh, there were more—lots more. I was actually being kind. So are you ready to get started?"

"Started with what?" I asked.

"Being a better version of yourself."

"Or not!" I said, taking off the sunglasses. Better Bertie had vanished. "See you later, loser," I mumbled. I quickly realized that I was calling myself a loser, and felt incredibly dumb.

Ping. I got a text from my mom.

ok 2 come up 2 mac's room now

I read it again. What would I be coming up to? Mac still asleep? Tabitha giving me the evil eye? Howard crying a million tears? As I pondered my next move, things got really-really strange.

The chapel turned dark and menacing. Winds from

71

nowhere whipped at my hair, and the walls literally started to close in.

But worst of all was the weight. I felt a gigantic sadness pushing down on my shoulders, the same crushing sadness I experienced my first night in Altoona. The pressure was so overwhelmingly powerful I could hardly move.

"AHHH!" I screamed.

Struggling to lift my hand, I put on the hoodoo glasses.

The air settled

The walls went still.

The weight lifted from me.

The chapel was beautiful and bright once again.

Swallowing a breath, I got my bearings.

Better Bertie stood close to me, smiling and glowing.

"That was you?" I asked, amazed by Better Bertie's ability to make her point. "The wind and the pressure and the wall thing?"

"Told you I was gonna blow your mind," she said.

16

Three Words

Stepping into an empty elevator, I pressed the "five" button to the ICU with my thumb.

"So what's the story with these sunglasses? And who was that lady in the chapel?" I looked at Better Bertie beside me.

"All of your questions will be answered when the time is right," she said. "But you might not like some of the answers."

Ding. Fifth floor.

As we entered the ICU, I gasped in shock. Better Bertie wasn't the only one glowing. I stopped to stare at all the radiant people coming and going. Nurses, an orderly, various visitors, and an old woman hobbling past us with a walker; they all glowed.

"Freaky, huh?" Better Bertie said. All I could do was silently nod. "They're auras," she said, walking two steps ahead

of me. "Everyone and everything that's alive has a certain …
energy. The higher the energy, the brighter the aura."

"I love it. I mean, I really love it!" I said, watching the
human light shows.

"What's that, young lady?"

The old woman with the walker, her aura a dull pea soup
green, glared at me. "Did you just say you love me?"

I hesitated, then said, "Well, yes."

The woman scoffed. But as she shuffled onward, her aura
bloomed into a shiny emerald green. Better Bertie patted
me on the back. "You're a lot smarter than your report cards
suggest, Bertie." No one heard her but me.

My smile faded.

Up ahead, Tabitha stood outside of Mac's room, texting
on her phone. The glow around her was a dark swirl of purple
and black.

Better Bertie must've read my thoughts. "Everyone has
a story," she said. "You think you know who Tabitha is, but
you don't know squat. And Tabitha has no idea who you are,
either."

I gestured to Tabitha's aura.

"Well, I know she's all dark and stormy. Look at her, it's
like she's full of lightning and hail, and maybe a tornado and
a tsunami."

74

"Uh, and so are you," said Better Bertie, pointing at my hands.

She was right. I had a cloudy dark purple aura, just like Tabitha.

That was when two storm fronts collided.

"Perfect. Now you're talking to yourself and wearing sunglasses indoors," Tabitha said. "Playing the crazy card, Bernice? I'm not buying *one minute* of your weirdo act. Why don't you do us all a favor and hop a bus to North Carolina."

Harsh! I was dying to launch a counterattack at Tabitha, but Better Bertie stopped me. "Don't do it," she said. "There's a healthier way of communicating your thoughts and feelings."

Against my better judgment, I said nothing. Tabitha scowled, and strode past us to a bathroom down the hall. Better Bertie smiled at me. "That went well."

My aura grew darker. I could feel it change.

"Yeah, for Tabitha maybe. Not for me."

"No, for you, too," Better Bertie said.

"Whatever," I said. "Just tell me how I get out of this disaster."

"You don't," she said.

"What? I thought you were here to help me!"

"I am. None of this is an accident."

"Oh, don't even go there."

"I'm already there. And so are you, you just don't know it yet. There's no getting out of this," Better Bertie said. "The quicker you make peace with that fact, the quicker you'll find out how you can help Mac. First, you have to stop lying to yourself and to everyone else, and maybe you should admit that Tabitha is no different from you."

"Dude, you're more nuts than I am! That girl is nothing like me. In fact, Tabitha and I could not be more different."

"Do you want my help or not, Bertie?"

"Sure. But you're doing a lousy job."

"Okay, fine. Try this," Better Bertie said, not missing a beat. "Say something mean about Tabitha. Anything you want, just as long as it's really-really horrible."

Mean thoughts ran through my head.

"Check it out. Tabitha is a total stupid jerk-face idiot who smells like dirty diapers and dog farts. How was that? Pretty good, right?"

"Excellent. Now say it again, only this time add three words, 'just like me.'"

"Okay. Tabitha is a total stupid jerk-face idiot who smells like dirty diapers and dog farts … just like me," I said. "No, that doesn't work anymore."

Better Bertie ignored me.

"Now say something nice about Tabitha, and add the

three words."

"Okay. Tabitha can sometimes be not too overly disgusting, just like me." As I said those words, the aura around me lightened. It wasn't much, but it felt good.

Better Bertie smiled. "It's amazing how much brighter things can be when you look at them differently."

Just then, I spotted my mom stepping out of Mac's room. She waved me closer.

"Time to go see Mac," I whispered to Better Bertie.

"You know what you need to say. Or you will know." She looked a bit too pleased with herself.

"Other me? You're getting on my *last* nerve," I said.

I took off the sunglasses. Better Bertie disappeared.

I turned toward Mac's room. Now what? What in the world was I going to say to those people, and to zonked-out Mac?

17

Attack!

My mom and Howard waited for me to say something. But my focus was on Mac. His eyes closed from the coma, he looked so broken. Surgical tape was everywhere, and a tube protruded from his skull to reduce the fluid in his brain. It wasn't the boy I was getting to know lying in the bed. No, it was more like a shattered porcelain doll someone had tried to glue together, but they had done a lousy job.

Water rose in my eyes. My stomach dropped. I thought again… *I'm the horrible thing that happened.* Now, Mac might never wake up.

I'd forgotten to breathe. My lungs burned for air. Taking in a deep breath, words began to flow from my mouth. I had no clue where these words were coming from, but they felt right. They felt … freeing.

"Seeing you this way, Mac, I ... there's something I want to do. I want to take away your pain, and tell you how sorry I am for everything. Sorry for saying all the stupid stuff I said these last nine days. I've just been so scared lately. But that's no excuse, Mac. I don't have any excuses to give you. I kicked the soccer ball across the street, and told you 'go fetch it.'" I teared up, overcome by what I had done. Before I could chicken out, I added, "Nothing will ever change those facts."

Tears made my vision streaky. My voice cracked as I touched Mac's hand, all his broken parts held together with rolls of mummy bandages. "If I could change what I did, Mac, I would. I'd do anything, *anything at all.* Tabitha was right. I should be in that bed, not you."

Head to toe, my body twitched like a frightened rabbit.

Stepping forward, Howard said, "Thank you, Bertie."

Another voice, this one filled with venom, interrupted our moment. "Don't let Bertie fool you, Dad. If her lips are moving, she's lying." Tabitha appeared in the doorway behind us.

Howard tightened. "We're not doing this again, Tabitha. We talked—"

"Bertie has done nothing but cause trouble since she got here. She's even trying to break you guys up so she can go back to North Carolina."

"Stop!" Howard said, seeming more irritated than angry.

But Tabitha didn't stop. Instead, she pointed at me. "I bet she gets what she wants now. Hope you're happy, Bernice!"

"Enough, Tabitha!" Howard was losing his temper.

Tabitha's eyes were like daggers. I stared bullets back.

"You think this is an act?" I asked.

"Wanna know what I think?" Tabitha spat through gritted teeth, her eyes a mix of tears and fury. "I think you're the *worst person* I ever met!"

I'm not going to lie, I wanted to punch Tabitha. But another part of me knew she was protecting her family. "Family is everything, the bees, the hive, and the honey," Great-aunt Tillie used to say. "Mess with any of those things, you should expect to get stung." I never really understood what she meant, not the full picture, until right then.

Seeing Tabitha this way, I realized that Better Bertie was right. Tabitha and I were much more alike than different.

Tabitha was hurting, just like me. Even though I understood that on one level, on another and more immediate level, I still wanted to punch her. Like really knock her out.

Unfortunately, she wasn't done telling me how rotten I was. "Nobody wants you here! Grab your *ugly, stinky, dumb dog* and go home to North Carolina today!"

A fierce blast of rage shot up my spine and into my brain.

All I could think to say was, "You total jerk-face idiot!"

Stalking toward Tabitha, my sunglasses slid down onto my nose. She came at me, defiant and ready. Her aura was all splotchy black and fiery red. Her pupils were sparks of steaming lava. *Okay, this is really going to happen*, I thought.

Tabitha and I were two high-speed trains on one track, about to collide head-on.

No stopping us now.

As Tabitha reared back to hit me, I threw a punch.

Howard vaulted between us.

Thump-thump.

"Ow!"

Howard got blasted from both sides.

18

The World's Stupidest Girl

"**I** cannot believe that happened!" Mom scolded me on the way back to Howard's house.

Tabitha and Howard were spending the night at the hospital. They wanted to be there in case there were any developments with Mac.

"You heard Tabitha," I said. "She's the one who started it."

"Really? You're going with 'she started it?' That's your best defense, huh?"

I didn't answer. My father told me that if you commit a crime, the best defense is silence. The second best defense is insanity. I had both of those covered.

Mom was so mad I thought her head might explode.

"What were you thinking, Bertie? Please tell me! One minute I'm literally in tears because I'm so amazed by you and

82

your kind, thoughtful words. What you said to Mac, trust me, I know that wasn't easy. But you didn't hide from it. You didn't lie. You took responsibility. And then the next minute? WHAM! I'm in tears because I'm so ashamed of you."

She was right—I was guilty. But I couldn't stay silent. "I want to tell you that I'm sorry, but I've said it so much already, it probably doesn't mean anything."

"Bingo!" she said.

"Mom, my brain, it's just not working right."

"Yeah, well neither is Mac's. That poor boy is fighting for his life, Bertie, while you're fighting his poor sister. Unacceptable! You have to do better."

We drove in awful silence for ten minutes. Finally, Mom turned our Volvo into the Mortons' driveway. In the moonlight I saw balloons, teddy bears, and "get well" cards waiting for us on the stoop of Howard's house. Kind gestures of hope from neighbors and friends of the Mortons. One part of me was grateful, but another part of me felt even guiltier.

Mom and I gathered the gifts and took them inside the house. Turning away from me, Mom phoned Howard on her cell. I sat on the stoop. Pulling out the sunglasses, I put them on and looked around, but I didn't see anything different. *Did they only work in the hospital? Has Better Bertie given up on me?* My thoughts ran wild.

83

Better Bertie was suddenly sitting so close to me, we nearly overlapped.

I jumped, startled, even though I should've been used to her coming and going. Better Bertie didn't say a word, just looked at me.

"What? Are you not talking to me, either?" I asked.

"Why bother?" she said. "You don't need me. You know everything already. Nobody can help you, girlfriend, if you don't want to be helped."

I groaned.

"It's not just me," Better Bertie said, motioning to the starry sky above us. "The universe is also trying to help you."

"Could've fooled me! If that's true, why do I feel so crappy all the time?"

"For starters, you talk too much, but you don't listen enough."

"I'm listening now. What's the universe trying to help me with? Tell me!"

"Honestly, I believe it has big plans for you, Bertie. Big-big plans. But before that can happen, you need to fix your broken heart."

That shut me up.

My heart felt broken ever since my parents got divorced. Or before that, when I knew my family was falling apart.

And now, with what had happened to Mac, my heart was basically a million pieces of broken glass. Unfixable.

"There are things going on right this second that we cannot see," Better Bertie said. "It's like gravity. Even though it's invisible, it's here." She took my hand. "Everything that's happening is happening for a reason. Greater forces are in play. Signs and wonders and mysteries. Hardwired connections between people and events that will only become evident when you are ready to see them."

"Really? Prove it," I said. "Have the universe show me a shooting star. No wait, *five* shooting stars. Then you'll get my full attention."

"Five shooting stars? Dude, I don't control the universe. It responds when it responds, and only with what's needed. You don't need to see five shooting stars."

"Ha! Guess you're not so much better than me after all, are you?" I said.

"And you wonder why people give you the silent treatment."

"Okay, we're done here. I've had enough of people insulting me for one day. And Leon needs some love and kibble. Nighty-night!" I took off the glasses. She was gone.

Instantly, a swirling gust of wind kicked up.

Whipping about, it buffeted my clothes and hair. Then I saw it. The wind swept the pink soccer ball I had booted across the street, over the road and into the Mortons' yard. The ball tumbled across the grass and banged to a spot at my feet. It was undeniably freaky. The ball, or the universe, was trying to get my attention.

Bending down, I grabbed the soccer ball and inspected it. "Oh my God, it can't be." The ball I was holding was not my ball. My soccer ball had my name on it, written in permanent ink.

It hit me all at once: I was the world's stupidest girl. Dangerous and prone to outbursts. I wanted to destroy the soccer ball, like it was to blame for Mac's accident. Instead, I put it inside the garage. Feeling awful and alone, I slid the glasses on, but Better Bertie didn't appear.

Where was she? I needed someone to talk to. Anyone.

While Mom was locking up Howard's optometry office, I went to the kennel to fill Leon's food bowl. With the glasses on, Leon glowed, a pale shade of gold. Whenever he pumped his tail back and forth, his aura got a little bit brighter. No wonder people love to watch a dog wag its tail.

I kept hoping Better Bertie would pop up and say something smart or helpful, but no. Though I didn't want to admit it, my heart was empty without her. A big hole.

Putting my pride aside, I called out to her. "Please don't leave me or give up on me, Better Bertie. I know I'm messed up, but I'm not a lost cause just yet. Who knows? I might surprise you. Are you here, Better Bertie?"

Silence. Until Leon farted.

"That was not the cosmic response I was hoping for," I said.

"Leon? I've never screwed up this badly before. Mac is in big trouble because of me. It's like the whole world around me is broken, and I don't know how to fix any of it. Better Bertie said the universe wants to help me, but I'm not so sure. I mean, why would the universe care about me? I'm just a lost, dopy girl from a small town. Nothing special." I stopped myself. Leon's tail was wagging like crazy. He was looking at the sky, and his aura was getting brighter. Following his gaze, I looked up. A shooting star streaked across the sky.

Then, blazing from the opposite direction, a second shooting star.

And a third shooting star

A fourth shooting star.

And a fifth.

The stars were just getting started.

All at once, a thousand shooting stars shot every which way.

The thrill was so overwhelming, it knocked me backward onto my butt.

The universe and Better Bertie had put on a show just for me. But I wasn't quite sure if I deserved it.

19

When Your House is on Fire

The next morning, I woke up at dawn feeling that same starry thrill. The same joy. Rushing downstairs, I made breakfast. My mom's favorite, French toast.

Putting everything on a tray, I went to her room. Through the half-open door, I saw her looking at a photo on her laptop of Howard, herself, Tabitha, Mac, and me. Everyone smiling, except for me. Covering her face, Mom cried. "So much for a fresh start."

My joy flew out of me. I was a Bertie Blount bomb that went off. And everybody around me got wounded by the blast.

Wheeling around, I brought the tray back to the kitchen. This wasn't going to be a breakfast-in-bed kind of day. Instead, I laid breakfast out on the table, and I waited.

"French toast? Nice, Bertie," my mother said five minutes

later when she stepped into the kitchen. She had composed herself. She even smiled as if it were a normal morning. I kept waiting for her interrogation, a hundred questions about the accident. But Mom didn't ask me anything. And even stranger, she didn't threaten to punish me.

Was she using reverse psychology? I decided to reverse her reversal.

"Should we talk about the accident and my punishment?" I asked.

"Why? What good will that do anyone?" Mom said.

"Well, I-I-I don't know, but …"

She cut me off. "Right now, the house is on fire. And when your house is on fire, you don't stop to look at who or what caused the flames, you just put out the fire. That's why Howard and I are not discussing it with you. But make no mistake, young lady, we will. And we will discuss it *in full*."

For a second, I thought she had done reverse-reverse-reverse psychology on me. But then it made sense. Number one: Put out the fire. Number two: Arrest the arsonist. Number three: Toss her in prison for a hundred years.

Gesturing, my mother said, "Where did you get those sunglasses? Are they the ones your great-aunt Tillie gave you?"

Unsure how to answer, I went with the truth. "These? No. The universe gave me these glasses, actually."

Mom darkened. "Do I look like I'm in the mood for clever answers?"

Before I could say anything, Mom's phone played a Mariah Carey song,

"You and I must make a pact, we must bring salvation back. Where there is love, I'll be there…"

That was Howard's ringtone. "I'll Be There" was Howard's and Mom's song.

She answered. The call was quick, less than a minute. After my mom put away her phone, she said, "Mac's still in critical condition. It's still touch and go."

I cursed under my breath. Why wasn't Mac improving? Did we need to find some better doctors or ship him to a better hospital?

Mom did not wait for my response. Turning away, she said, "I'll be leaving for the hospital in ten minutes.

"Okay, great. I'll get dressed," I said, following her down the hall.

"No need for that, you're staying home today," she said. "Clean up around here. Tidy up your room, and maybe think about how you can be a better team player."

"But Mom, I need to be at the hospital."

She shook her head. "You being there will only make things worse."

Mom's words stung like an attack of angry hornets. I fought crying, and I fought saying mean things back. *Fine,* I thought. *If no one wants me at the hospital, no problem.* I won't have to deal with stupid Tabitha or weepy Howard. Leon and I will hang out and watch Netflix all day. Or, even better, we will run away somewhere where people want us around.

But then I wondered what Better Bertie would want me to do. *Watch Netflix* or *run away* was not the answer that popped into my head.

"Mom, I have to be at the hospital," I repeated.

She looked at me eye-to-eye.

"It's not a good idea. More of Mac's relatives will be at the hospital this afternoon. They may not say it, Bertie, but they'll be looking for someone to blame. That means they'll be looking at me and they'll be looking at you. The *me* I can take." Mom tapped her chest. "The *you* I cannot."

"Mom? It's super important that I go to the hospital with you."

"Are you not hearing me? This is not about you, Bertie. For once, can you please just listen and not argue? Just do as you are told."

"I am listening. Mac's family may say some mean stuff to me. I get it, and I'll just take it. I don't really care what they say or do."

"Well, I do. And I can't always be there to protect you."

"Mac needs protection more than I do. I'm the reason he's at the hospital, and I … I need to find a way to help him get better. So I have to be at the hospital!"

Her hand gently cupped my face as she smiled and looked into my eyes. "How can you help Mac?"

"I don't know, but I feel like I'm supposed to do something. Please let me go with you, Mom. We are a package deal, right?"

"And if Tabitha or someone else says something harsh, what happens then?"

I hesitated, unsure of how to respond. Then suddenly I came up with an answer Mom couldn't argue with.

"Then I feed the right wolf," I said, holding my breath and waiting for her to agree to let me go see Mac.

"Clever answer," Mom said, her voice softening ever so slightly.

"Let me go, Mama. I promise I'll be good."

"You better," Mom jerked her thumb toward the stairs, "Get dressed. You got five minutes before the Volvo leaves."

Running to my room, I peeled off my pajamas and threw on some clothes. But as I dashed down the hall, something stopped me. Gravity or some other unseen force pulled me inside Mac's bedroom. The room of the boy I had nearly killed.

Surveying his walls and shelves, I decided to put on the

sunglasses. Maybe Better Bertie would have some answers or advice.

The room came alive, just like I was hoping it would. I didn't see Better Bertie, but everything had a glow to it, except for a pair of leather dress shoes that I imagined pinched Mac's growing feet. Near his bed, a stack of comic books glowed like nightlights. They weren't all that different from the manga and anime I liked.

Then I saw something glowing red through the nylon fabric of a backpack hanging on a wall hook. Opening a pocket, I pulled out a red Hot Wheels race car that shone much brighter than everything else. I placed it on Mac's desk.

"Bertie, it's time!" Mom called from downstairs.

"Be right there," I yelled.

Before I could leave the bedroom, the red race car started doing loops across Mac's desk. No joke. After three loops, the car did a tight three-sixty around a pencil cup, then it stopped in the middle of the desk as if it were proud of itself.

"I'm guessing Mac really loves that toy car," I said, astonished.

A voice sounded behind me. "You are an excellent guesser."

Whipping around, I saw Better Bertie sitting on Mac's bed. "Do you want to help Mac, Bertie? Do you *really* want to help him?"

"Yes! I'll do anything!"

"Great. How are you gonna do it?" Better Bertie asked.

"What do you mean, how? You're the one with all the answers!"

"Well, what do you think would be most useful to Mac?"

"Not you, obviously. What is this, are you trying to make me mad?"

"I'm trying to make you think, Bertie. If I just tell you stuff, it won't stick. You need to puzzle things out for yourself. What is the *one* thing Mac needs more of? Think. It's what everyone needs. You even heard it on Mom's phone this morning."

"Mom's phone?" I said, confused.

Better Bertie sang Mom and Howard's tune. "*Where there is love, I'll be there.*"

"Stop singing! Love's not gonna work for me, dude. I stink at love."

"Because you keep pushing it away."

"Whatever! I don't have time to get all soul-searchy with you now. Mom's waiting."

I turned for the door, but Better Bertie jumped in front of me.

"If you don't start thinking differently, Bertie, *nothing* will change. Instead of listening to your head, try listening to your heart. You'll be amazed at what can happen."

"BERTIE, NOW!" Mom shouted, from downstairs.

20

Thinking Differently

Mom drove us to the hospital, a little too fast and a little too furious. Some guy in a souped-up muscle car cut in front of us, and mom pounded the horn. "Hey, are you blind? Idiot!"

Angry hearts run in my family.

As we neared the hospital entrance, I thought about what Better Bertie had told me. If I didn't start thinking differently, nothing would change.

I tasted desperation in my mouth. Things needed to change. The old way wasn't working. So I decided to give it a go. I worked up a head of steam. *Let's do this.*

Okay, this is me thinking differently. Being better.

"Mom. I really love you," I said, touching her arm.

She said nothing for a few seconds.

Then she glanced at me, distracted. "Sorry, did you say something?"

"Uh, just that I like your hair," I said, losing my confidence but not my nervousness nor my self-doubt. I was gonna screw up things up again, I just knew it.

Howard and Tabitha were in the ICU's waiting area when we arrived.

Howard wrapped my mom up in a hug, and then he smiled at me. It looked totally forced. I was probably the last person in the world he wanted to see.

"Any news?" Mom asked.

Howard shook his head. "Afraid not. No changes." He cleared his throat, which was apparently a signal to Tabitha. She came up to me after I had taken a seat.

"Sorry about the fight and everything else that happened yesterday," she said in a quiet voice. "I was just upset about Mac being hurt. I didn't mean any of that stuff I said."

Howard must've told Tabitha to apologize.

"Me, too," I said. "I'm sorry for what I said. I need to think differently. I need to be better."

Tabitha offered me her hand. We shook hands. Then, without another word, Tabitha returned to her seat and watched the TV, which was showing a black and white World War II movie. I suspected the war between Tabitha and me wasn't over.

But for Mac's sake, at least, we had a temporary ceasefire.

Opening my backpack, I surveyed the bizarro contents inside. There was a pair of hexed sunglasses, a haunted cellphone, and now Mac's enchanted toy metal car. I almost felt like a wizard, toting around magical gear. All that was missing was a wand and one of those goofy, old school wizard hats that look like bent purple traffic cones.

A few minutes later, I went down the hall to Mac's room. Feeling a dark presence, I turned and saw Tabitha watching me in the doorway. Arms crossed, eyes narrowed. I didn't need trippy shades to know that Tabitha's aura had gone dark and cold. She came at me like an arctic wind, blocking my path.

"You're not going in there." She motioned to Mac's room.

"Tabitha, I want to help."

"Now that it's just you and me, I am *not* sorry about one thing I said to you. You're selfish and stupid, and I can't stand the sight of your ugly face."

"Please tell me how you really feel," I said.

"Know this, Bernice, I'm gonna get you. One way or another, I will ruin you, just like you ruined Mac. That's a promise."

And with that, Tabitha marched off.

So yeah, the war was not over. The ceasefire had lasted a whole ten minutes.

21

Someone Else's Nikes

M orton family relatives arrived from all over the state and country. The waiting room was packed with them. I met the parents of Mac and Tabitha's late mother, Sandra. They'd flown in from Nebraska, I think. Howard introduced Mom and me to his brother Dennis, three of his cousins, and a bunch of aunts, uncles and in-laws.

I had to give Tabitha props. She'd kept her word about ruining me.

I spotted Tabitha whispering to different relatives, then I saw them look accusingly in my direction. Narrowed eyes. Hateful scowls. Folded arms and shaking heads. Bottom line, Tabitha was telling them I was to blame for Mac's accident.

"Think differently," I kept telling myself. But I could feel dark emotions rising up inside me. Morton relatives gave me phony smiles and asked me phony questions about my life, but deep down I knew they wanted to clobber me with a big stick. It's like the waiting room was filled with dynamite, and I was the lit fuse.

Desperate not to explode, I ducked inside the bathroom and put on the sunglasses. I needed Better Bertie. And there she was, laughing at me in the big mirror.

"Wow-wee, girl, you look awful," Better Bertie said.

"Really? You're going there, right off?" I huffed.

Better Bertie wasn't finished. "Seriously, look at yourself. If guilt and shame got married and they had a disaster baby, it would look exactly like you."

"Hey Miss Congeniality, you got a point, or what?"

"Yep, quit hating yourself. It doesn't help you, Mac, or anybody else, Bertie. It just puts pimples on your soul."

"Is that really a thing, soul pimples?" I said.

"There's an old saying," Better Bertie said as she exited the mirror ghost-style. It was fantastically cool, but she played it off like it was no biggie. "To understand someone else, you have to stand in their penny loafers."

She motioned. "Check out your new kicks."

Looking down, I gasped. Somehow, I had on a shiny pair of men's loafers, easily size 14. They looked so big, I might as well have been wearing the box they came in.

99

Then something even more bizarre happened. The mirror turned into a window—a magic one. On the other side of it, Howard talked with his brother Dennis while they sat in the hospital cafeteria. Howard was wearing the same shiny Bigfoot loafers as me.

Now things got even more bizarre. I could hear Howard's thoughts.

They were scattered and harsh. He wasn't listening to Dennis blathering on about the Pittsburg Pirates batting order. Howard was having his own inner argument. *This is all my fault. I was stupid for thinking we could have a true family again. Mac will never forgive me, if he ever has the chance to. How did I let it get so wrong?*

Listening to Howard's tortured thoughts, I realized something. "He means me, doesn't he?" I glanced at Better Bertie. "I'm the wrong thing, right?"

For the first time, Better Bertie looked unsure. Sad, even.

"No, Bertie, what you're hearing isn't Howard hating on you. Truth is, he's hating on himself. He's racked with guilt about Mac's accident."

"Why? The accident was my fault, not Howard's. He didn't do anything wrong."

"You're the one standing in his loafers. You tell me why he feels guilty."

When I looked at Howard through the mirror, cold, heavy air rushed at me all at once. I felt Howard's pain. A regret so sharp and deep my body ached. His thoughts came to me like a scroll across my mind.

"For three years he's been a single parent running a busy optometry practice. He spent so much time at the office, he's had no ... almost no time for his kids. He wanted to be a better father. He wanted to give ... give his family a fresh start after his wife passed away. But it's too late. His beautiful little boy is dying and he can't ... he can't stop it. And even though he truly loves my mom, he knows he has to ... he has to send her away."

Tears fell from under my glasses. They were both mine and Howard's. It was exhausting: My mind and body were wiped out. Blowing out a long breath, I looked at Better Bertie. "Stop it. I don't want to do this anymore."

"Too bad, girlfriend, we are not done," she said. "But you do look pretty in pink."

She motioned to my feet once again. Peering down, I saw Howard's loafers had been replaced by Tabitha's pink Nikes that were a size too small. Looking into the magical window, I watched Tabitha as she sat beside Mac's bed.

"Tell me what you hear," Better Bertie said.

There was absolutely no way I wanted to know what was

going inside Tabitha's mind, but her thoughts came at me anyway. And they shocked me even more than Howard's thoughts. "This is so wrong!" I said. "Tabitha thinks Mac's accident was her fault?"

"In a way, yes." Better Bertie nodded. "But Tabitha's guilt is more complicated. Mostly, she regrets letting Mac chase after the soccer ball. As the older sister, she feels it was her job to have stopped him, or that she should have challenged you to fetch the ball since you were the one who kicked it. That's why Tabitha is so determined to challenge you now."

The words hit me like a wrecking ball.

"There's more," Better Bertie said. "Look." She pointed to Tabitha in the magic window.

"You are all we have now, Mac," Tabitha told her sleeping brother. "Dad's been busy working, trying to take care of us the best way he can now that Mom is gone. I'll take care of you. I'll protect you. I won't let anyone or anything hurt you, I promise. So please wake up so we can get on with our lives, okay?" Tabitha kissed Mac's forehead, and stared lovingly at him.

A wave of emotions hit me—hard. Heavy truths walloped me, too.

"After their mother died, Tabitha took on the mom role for Mac," I told Better Bertie. "Since Howard was constantly at work, Tabitha took charge. She packed their school lunches and helped Mac with his homework. She even did their laundry. She felt it was her duty to protect her brother. So she made it her life's mission to do just that. And she'd failed, miserably. If she hadn't failed, Mac would be running around, riding his bike, and playing with his Hot Wheels cars, not lying half-dead on a hospital bed."

Watching Tabitha clutch Mac's hand, I got a whole-body heartache. It took all my strength not to fly into a fit of ugly sobs. Turns out, I'm not that strong. Two breaths later, that's exactly what I did: boogers-out-the-nose sobbing.

Tabitha. That horrible, rotten girl who swore she'd ruin me, maybe wasn't so bad after all. I wanted to hug her. Though I knew if I got too close, she'd happily drop-kick me out the door.

The magic window flashed back to a normal mirror a second before the bathroom door opened. In it, I spied my mother's reflection.

"Bertie, I've been looking all over for you," she said.

Quickly, I set my sunglasses down, and washed my hands so Mom couldn't see my magnificent hot mess of a booger face. Swallowing a frantic breath, I cleared my throat to sound normal. "Everything okay?" My voice cracked.

"That depends." She held up her iPhone. "Your father wants to talk to you."

22

Massaging the Truth

"Have the police asked you any questions?" Dad asked. I was talking to him on Mom's cell. I'd hurried down the elevator and outside the hospital so I'd have privacy in case we talked about escape and rescue plans. Happy and sad at once. Pacing back and forth.

"No. They just talked to Howard and Mom, I think."

"That's good. If the cops do interview you or an insurance investigator starts poking around, do not in any way suggest that you are to blame for the accident."

"What? No, Daddy, they know. I told them all it was my fault."

"I don't care what you already said. Not another word to the police, the doctors, or anybody else. Okay?"

It almost felt like I had been smacked.

"You want me to lie to the police?" I said.

"It's not lying, it's legalese," he said. "Sometimes we have to massage the truth to get to the truth. And the truth is that Mac ran into the street without due regard for his life or personal safety."

"Wow. That sounds like an example of legalese."

"This is how it has to be. Even if you told Mac to fetch the ball, which you will never again admit to doing, he made the decision to do it. Understand?"

"No."

"Bertie, if Mac's father sues your mom and me, we could lose everything, including your college fund," Dad said. "So go along with the game plan, got it?"

"Can you just come here? I need you here now, Daddy. I can't think straight."

"No, not for another day, yet. I'm sorry."

"Are you real-real sorry?"

"What?"

"Nothing. Never mind."

Talking to my dad has always been one of my all-time favorite things to do. We could cover any topic. From deep-space exploration to deep-sea diving and everything in between. He was so good at talking, he could convince me of anything. But this conversation crushed me. It hurt in unexpected places. I could actually feel pain in my hair. My toenails, too. Everything was wrong.

As Dad continued to coach me, I reached for the sunglasses atop my head so I could check in with Better Bertie, but they weren't there. I went through my pockets. Not there, either. I rummaged through my backpack with my free hand. Nope. My panic level erupted. I needed Better Bertie. *Now.*

"Just so we are clear, Bertie, if this thing goes to court, I want you to say that the soccer ball landed on the other side of the street," my dad said. "And Mac, without any encouraging and before either you or Tabitha could stop him, recklessly chased after it."

"Please don't keep talking about the accident, Daddy. I can't lie, I just can't. I've already got too many pimples on my soul."

"Pimples on your what?" I could hear his voice shift into closing arguments mode. "Listen to me, Peach Pie. I know that this is adult stuff, and it's terrible. So let me handle it. Trust me, okay? I've handled hundreds of accident cases. When young kids are involved, things can get complicated very quickly, especially when the doctors aren't certain of a recovery. From now on, I need you to stay out of Mac's hospital room."

"Shouldn't be a problem," I said. "The Mortons don't want me there, either."

"Perfect. Tomorrow night I will be there, okay?" My father loved courtroom theatrics, even in real life. He'd clearly been saving this part for last. "And when I get there, I'm taking you to Carver City with me. I'm bringing you home, sweetheart!"

The world stopped.

I stopped.

The words I had literally prayed to hear since Mom and Leon and me arrived in Altoona, had finally been spoken.

I should've shouted with joy. I should've done backflips. Instead, I was worried that I had lost my sunglasses.

"Did you hear me, Bertie?" Dad asked. "Tomorrow night I am bringing you home! Doesn't that sound good? What do you have to say?"

I opened my mouth, but no words came out. Over the hospital's outside speakers, a voice sounded. "Bernice Blount, please report to the first-floor nursing desk."

"Great, Daddy. Thanks. See you tomorrow. Love you!"

Clicking END CALL, I dashed inside the hospital.

23

Tug of War

The two nurses at the front desk were super busy. They shook their heads at me. "No, there was no page," one of them said. Clearly, they did not want to deal with a kid. "Trust me, we would know," the other nurse said.

"But I heard it, I did!" I protested. "The page said 'Bernice Blount, please report to the first-floor nursing desk.' That's me, I'm Bernice, but I can't stand that name, so everyone calls me Bertie, unless they're mad at me. And lately, people have been calling me Bernice a lot. Anyway, there was a page, and it was a female voice."

The taller nurse drummed her fingers on the desk. "I'm the one who makes the pages, and I promise you, I did not page anyone, *Bernice*."

She was not getting rid of me that easily. Someone had

paged me. Someone had wanted me to come here. I had to figure out who and why, and fast. "Did anyone turn in a pair of lost sunglasses?" I asked.

Both nurses rolled their eyes. Digging out a cardboard box marked "Lost and Found," the shorter nurse plopped it on the desk. "Make it quick."

I searched the box. Ratty jackets, sweaty hats, a ripped crossword puzzle book, a pair of socks, some gloves, a stuffed animal, but no sunglasses.

Sliding the box back, I sighed. "Thanks anyway."

The nurses seemed ecstatic to be done with me so they could talk about a hot doctor they both wanted to date.

Turning away, my face flushed red and my skin felt prickly. In my mind's eye I saw something strange. The crossword puzzle book from the "Lost and Found" box. The front cover was ripped just enough to reveal the first puzzle, and a secret message meant only for my eyes.

I had to get that book. Turning, I said, "Wait, can I see the box again?"

The taller nurse was just now putting the box away. She gave me a look of contempt, and said, "Know what, kid? Go get your parents."

Out of desperation, I gripped the other side of the box. When the nurse pulled, I pulled. A tug of war.

RRRRIPPP!

The cardboard box tore in two. Jackets, hats, the crossword puzzle book, and a pair of gloves exploded everywhere.

Now I was certain the nurses hated me. The shorter one called security on a landline phone. "We have a young troublemaker at the front desk," she told someone.

Grabbing the crossword puzzle book, I quickly scanned the first puzzle. Someone had filled in only three answers to the clues: *ROOM … TRIPLE …* and *… CINCO.*

24

Room 555

Room Triple Cinco, also known as Room 555, was seven rooms down from Mac's room.

Avoiding the Morton relatives, I slipped down the hall. Glancing back to make sure no one was eyeballing me, especially my mom, I put an ear to the door and listened. It was quiet, so I went inside.

Room 555 was empty except for a bed with clean sheets, a table, and a chair. My sunglasses were on the bed. How did they get there? I had never been in that room until right then. Someone must've wanted me to find them. A rush of joy caused me to clap and bounce like I had won the grand prize on a TV game show.

I could not remember the last time I had bounced.

Eager to talk to Better Bertie, I put on the sunglasses. But she wasn't there.

Room 555 suddenly turned dark, except for a weak light near the ceiling.

A woman was lying on the bed, but I could hardly see her face.

A man with black hair was hunched over her, sobbing while holding her hand. They either didn't see me, or they were ignoring me.

My chest tightened. The woman's glow faded in and out. She was fading away. And I knew in that way people just know stuff, her light would soon be gone.

She was dying.

The man took the woman's hand as I blurted, "Oh my God! Howard, is that you?" Yes, it was Howard Morton. He had a beard and wore different clothing, but it was definitely Howard.

Fortunately, he couldn't hear me, for some reason. But who was the woman he was with?

"OH MY GOD!" I said even louder. An electrical charge ran from my feet to my hair when I realized who she was. The woman was Howard's wife, Sandra. His *dying* wife, and Tabitha and Mac's dying mom.

But how was I seeing something that had happened like three years ago? Had the glasses allowed me to time travel?

Smiling at Howard, Sandra said, "When I'm gone, you need to find someone."

I gulped. Being there was uncomfortable, watching a private and life-changing moment. Part of me wanted to sneak away, but it was like my tennis shoes were glued to the floor.

"I can't. I won't," Howard said. He leaned closer to his wife, then he sang an old love song to her. *"Let me be the one you come running to … I want to spend my whole life with you."*

He didn't make it any further. His voice caught.

"You're still a terrible singer." Sandra nearly laughed. I could tell she would've teased him some more had she not been in so much pain.

Her voice was weak, but it brimmed with warmth and compassion and love. "Howard, we only have a few moments left to go. Here's the deal. You need to find a new love song to share with someone else."

Howard shook his head. He clearly didn't want to hear her words, but Sandra kept talking.

"Listen to me now. Our kids are about to lose their mother, and it's your job …" She stopped, so she could cup Howard's face in her frail hands. "It's *your* job to teach Tabitha and Mac that life goes on. And I will always be with them, in their hearts. But they cannot make losing me their story, their reason for not moving forward and succeeding in life. You must be strong for them. Give them the family they need. The family you all deserve. That is the most important job you have right now. Do you understand?"

Howard could not answer. I thought I understood why. He was a train wreck of sadness, bitterness, and anger.

"Love our beautiful babies, Howard," Sandra said. "Take … good care of them."

With that, she closed her eyes. Soon after, her light faded away. The bedside monitor squealed an alarm. Howard cried out in such agony, I could not watch him any longer.

I tore off the sunglasses. Tears fell out of my eyes faster than I could thumb them away. And then anger seized me. I was fiercely mad at the doctors for not saving Sandra Morton's life, and for not saving Howard and his kids from getting swept away by a tidal wave of sadness and loss.

My anger grew stronger, and it sought new targets: Better Bertie and the universe. Why had they sent me—*tricked* me!—into going inside this room so I could witness such a heartbreaking scene between Howard and his dying wife? Yes, I had royally screwed up by booting the soccer ball across the street and telling Mac and Tabitha to fetch it. But this was too much of a penalty. Why did they force me to suffer along with Howard, who I barely knew, and his wife, who I did not know at all? Twenty years in jail would've been less harsh than seeing what I had just seen, a wife and a mother of two young kids losing her light.

I wanted to scream or run away from the hospital, destination unknown. Run until I dropped. Or curl up in a dark corner and shed every last tear I owned. But not a corner of Room 555. It was freaking me out again. Daylight streamed inside through a window. Howard and Sandra were gone. My time travel trip had ended. The room was empty, except for a bed with clean sheets, and a table and a chair.

And me.

Finally realizing who had given me the sunglasses, I left the haunted room and ran to the elevators, into a headwind, it seemed, like powerful forces were trying to keep me on the fifth floor. The floor where Sandra Morton died three years ago, and where her son Mac was fighting to stay alive that very day.

25

The Ghost I Had Come To See

D^{ing.}

The elevator reached the second floor. When I stepped out of it, planning to head to the chapel, I noticed that some people were watching me.

Sort of.

Standing directly in front of me were two hospital security guards holding tablet gizmos. The men were gazing at security camera footage of a familiar scene. It was me and the nurse from the first floor having our "Lost and Found" box tug of war. Apparently, I was a fugitive from justice. I had to fight laughing when the video showed the box ripping, and hats and gloves and the puzzle book, the whole shebang, flying everywhere.

If I giggled or made any movement at all, the guards

would probably glance up from their tablets and notice me standing in front of them. What to do?

I froze against the wall and put on the glasses.

The guards' auras were a harsh crimson and green. They looked like hunters tracking a deer. And I was cute little Bambi!

The Neck Tattoo Guard pointed at his tablet, which now displayed footage from a second security camera, showing me pressing an elevator floor button a dozen times, after I jumped inside the car.

"Suspect steals the crossword puzzle book, sees we're coming, runs to the elevators to avoid apprehension, and presses five. Looks like five."

Neck Tattoo's partner, Muscle Guy Guard, nodded. "Five it is!" With that, they both looked up, directly at me. Neck Tattoo's eyes narrowed. "Hey, wait a minute!"

The whole "deer in the headlights" thing is true. I wanted to run, but I couldn't move my legs. I stood there like a dummy as I waited to get busted. The guards reached for me, but then a row of overhead lights exploded. Shattered bits of glass rained down on the men, but not on me.

That was when things turned spooky.

POP-POP-POP!

A bunch of helium "get well" balloons a man was holding popped like gunfire.

CLANG-CLANG-CLANG!

The elevator doors banged open and shut like jaws on a shiny metal monster.

WHAM-CRASH-SMASH!

Six empty wheelchairs, moving on their own, slammed into the guards.

"Ow! What's going on here? An earthquake?" Neck Tattoo shouted.

I wanted to tell them it was actually a supernatural event, and that in the past ten days I had seen ghosts, dead people, a doppelganger, crows, omens, wolves, and lots of spooky things. Instead of speaking up, I watched the possessed wheelchairs chase the guards down the hall. It was hilarious, watching grown men run from empty wheelchairs.

I ran in the opposite direction.

Hot-stepping it down the hall, I again spotted the painted quote above the chapel's door. "*We are not human beings having a spiritual experience. We are spiritual beings having a human experience.*" Yesterday, I didn't understand it. Today, the message was starting to become a little bit clearer.

I went inside the chapel, hoping to find a ghost. I saw Tabitha instead.

She was seated by herself, near the candles. Dancing light flickered across her face. Her eyes were closed in prayer. I got a clear sense she did not know I was watching her pray aloud, like she had done in her bedroom during my first night in Pennsylvania.

"Dear Mom in heaven," Tabitha said. "If you can hear me, I desperately need your help. Mac's in big trouble, Mom. He's hurt bad, really bad, and he's getting worse. You always knew the right words to say and the best medicines to give us. So I need you to show up and help heal Mac. I tried to look after him since you died, but now I've screwed everything up. And I'm so scared he's going to die. I wouldn't be able to take it. I still can't believe I lost you, Mom. I can't lose Mac, too."

She sniffled and wept, and her voice stuttered.

"Mom? I know that I disappointed you sometimes. Well, quite often, actually." Tabitha paused, like she was searching for the right words. "And now it's too late to tell you how sorry I am. I wish I had been nicer to you, and I wish I had not caused so much trouble. But I need you to know I miss you, Mom. I miss you every hour of every day. Please come to this hospital and help Mac. I love you, Mom. Amen."

Tabitha stood, and walked over to the table with candles. She sighed a long, exasperated sigh, and then lit a candle.

She still didn't see me.

But I saw someone else. The ghost I had come to see was suddenly standing next to Tabitha, as if she had heard her daughter's prayer. Sandra Morton, Mac and Tabitha's ghost mother. I could smell her lavender perfume.

Tabitha had prayed to her dead mother in heaven, but now her mom was just inches away, giving her a sideways hug. It was beautiful. And incredibly sad. I was the only girl in the chapel who could see ghosts, thanks to the freaky sunglasses.

I thought about telling Tabitha her mom was with her. I thought again. Tabitha would say I was lying. She might even wallop me.

So, instead of getting into another fight, I slipped unseen out of the chapel. In the hallway, I got a text from my mom.

Come to Mac's room. NOW.

26

Witch's Wart

The hallway outside of Mac's room was frantic madness. Nurses and doctors swept in and out. Mom and Tabitha and Howard and the gang of Morton relatives, eleven or twelve of them, watched helplessly. They whispered, hugged, and prayed.

I stood a few feet from the group's edge. Safer that way. Every so often, I'd sneak a quick glance through my glasses. Whenever anyone in the Morton gang looked my way, their auras flashed dark and spiteful. Most of them ignored me. I wasn't a girl anymore. I was a hairy witch's wart they wanted to cut off.

Only fifteen minutes had passed, but it felt like fifteen hours.

Finally, Dr. Myles approached Howard, Mom, and Tabitha.

"The good news is that although Mac's seizures caused him to go into cardiac arrest, we were able to get his heart to resume normal function rather quickly. What's the bad news? Well, he's not yet out of the woods. The latest EKG is not what we had hoped to see, and the MRI results also concern us. But Mac is off the respirator, and he's breathing on his own."

Howard tried to smile, but it ended up looking like a wince. "What happens next?" he asked the doctor. "What's the plan?"

"We wait, we run more tests, and we hope to see signs of healing," Dr. Myles said. "I have to be honest, it could go the other way. If Mac's brain shuts down to what is sometimes referred to as a vegetative state, things could deteriorate rather rapidly. My best advice is that you should try to be prepared for all possibilities, good or bad."

Tabitha lost her breath. She glared at the ceiling like she was searching for her mother.

Howard's knees buckled. My mom wrapped an arm around him, doing her best to keep him strong and upright. I don't think anyone believed that their upcoming wedding would actually happen. It couldn't. Not unless Mac recovered.

I felt my blood burning, furious with myself. Every negative emotion I had ever owned burned hot inside me, waiting for the right moment to boil over and send me on a destructive rampage. The big problem? I didn't have a good target for my rage. It wasn't Dr. Myles' fault that Mac hadn't woken up yet, and wasn't getting better. It wasn't Howard's fault, or Tabitha's fault, or even the truck driver's fault. No, only I was to blame for this horrible and hurtful mess.

Sometimes the truth will crush you into dusty bits. Other times it will act like a fuel. In the middle of all that sorrow and brokenness, I told myself I had to do more to help Mac turn things around—somehow or some way—so he would wake up and open his eyes. And that meant I would need to ignore my father's order to stay far away from Mac's room.

"Sorry, Dad," I whispered to my absent father. "Maybe one of these days you'll understand and forgive me." I looked around and saw Tabitha's squinched eyes and pinched-up face. She was throwing more hatred and disgust my way. I just nodded and turned away, knowing I deserved her revulsion and even worse things.

27

Don't Buckle Up

Three Morton family members came out of Mac's room. The relatives had been visiting Mac for the last few minutes in groups of twos and threes. Now, most of them were talking to Howard and my mom in the hallway.

When Mac's room was empty, I snuck inside. I had to see Mac. There was something I needed to tell him.

Machines beeped and buzzed as I took a seat beside Mac's bed. I didn't think it was possible, but Mac looked even more frail and broken than he had yesterday.

I kissed Mac on his cheek, and blew air against his eyelashes.

"Do you still like weird stuff? 'Cause buddy, I got a whole bunch of weird for you to enjoy. I don't have much time, so I'll just share this. Your mom gave me a pair of sunglasses that let me see a better version of myself. Not a bad start, right?"

Mac didn't respond. The machines registered no change.

"So Better Bertie tells me that if I don't start thinking differently, nothing will change. The same ole, same ole will keep happening over and over. At first, I figured she was just trying to help me out. Better Bertie comes and goes, it's kind of annoying. Anyway, I think she wanted me to share the piece of advice about thinking differently with you, Mac."

No response, said the machines.

"Wherever you are, Mac, find a way out of there. You've gotta do it now, buddy. You don't have time to be afraid. Get bold. Get crazy. Just do it. Find a way to think different! Can you even hear me?"

No response.

I sat silently amid the machines. If anyone had heard the way I was talking to Mac, no doubt they would've told me I was being weird or inappropriate. I didn't care. I wanted Mac to fight.

Finally, I sighed and stood up. I left the little boy with one last incentive. "If you wake up for me, Mac, you can pet Leon whenever you want to, take him for walks, and treat him like he's your dog, too."

Still, no response. I was getting upset. At the machines. At Mac. And at Dr. Myles and God.

"Promise me you won't die, okay? You can't die, Mac. It's

125

not good for either of us. I put the only Morton who likes me in a coma. Sorry, bad joke."

Nothing changed with Mac.

Grabbing my backpack, I walked to the door. I stopped when I spotted something glowing in my backpack's side pocket. It looked like a burning red frog trying to bust out. Then I heard the *vroom vroom* of a car engine, and I remembered the Hot Wheels race car.

"No way!"

Digging out the tiny car, I placed it in Mac's left hand and folded his fingers around it. As soon as I let go of Mac's hand, the race car fell to the floor. But the feisty car would not be denied. Vroom vrooming louder, and spinning out on the floor tiles, it was like it wanted Mac to hold it.

I picked up the toy car and tried again.

"Grab the car, Mac," I whispered. "Wait, no! Even better, get inside the car, then hit the gas and drive yourself home. Do it, Mac. Drive yourself back to us!"

Finally, a response.

Glancing down, I saw Mac gripping the race car. Gripping it hard like it was a lifeline connecting him to the world of the living.

"Excuse us, Bernice, it's our turn now."

In the doorway, I saw a group of Mortons waiting to visit

with Mac. Each one of them, except for Howard's brother, Dennis, who was actually kind of friendly and cool, gave me the witch's wart look. Time to get out of here.

I bent down to Mac, and I whispered more inappropriate instructions into his ear.

"Drive fast during your journey home to us."

"Take chances."

"Ignore red traffic lights."

"Don't buckle up!"

28

Getting Busted Will Ruin Everything

I couldn't shake the security guards! Neck Tattoo and Muscle Guy Guard stepped off the elevator onto Mac's floor. Their heads swiveled this way and that way.

I spotted them from the waiting room. They would've spotted me, too, if it hadn't been for the Morton gang standing between us like a human forest. Five or six Mortons left the hospital. The other Mortons stayed behind and said they'd text the deserters if Mac's conditioned changed.

Using the Mortons' oversized bellies and butts as cover, I slipped away like a girl ninja down the hall.

Glancing back, I saw Neck Tattoo and Muscle Guy Guard making a path through the Morton forest. No way was I going to let those chuckleheads nab me. Mom's stress level was already at DEFCON One. Me getting busted by

128

hospital security guards would make her go nuclear.

The stairwell was the answer.

I speed-walked toward the door until someone grabbed me from behind.

Mom. Her eyes were wet but bright.

"What's wrong, Mom?"

"Nothing at all." She pulled me into an embrace. "Finally, a bit of good news!"

Howard and Tabitha were behind us. "Thank you, Tabby." Howard said to his daughter. "What a fantastic idea. You did such a wonderful thing.".

"Cool," Tabitha said, uncertain. "Now tell me what I did so I can do it again."

"The race car, Tabitha. You brought Mac's favorite Hot Wheels car to him. He's been holding it on his own. It's a huge step in the right direction."

"He is? That's great!" Tabitha beamed at the good news. "But I didn't bring his race car, Dad. It was probably one of the cousins who did that for Mac." She gave me a look that said, *speak up and take credit, and I will end your life.*

"Really?" Howard said, showing a skeptical look. "But which one?"

I didn't want to take credit for four reasons.

One: No one would believe me.

Two: I was just happy that they were happy, and that Mac was holding the car.

Three: I wasn't in the mood to be murdered by Tabitha.

Four: The security guards would be coming around the corner any second.

The stairwell was five steps away. Freedom, here I come.

"She did it." Uncle Dennis waddled out of Mac's room, pointing at me. "Bernice brought him the car. I saw her place it in Mac's hand."

"Is that true?" Howard said, stepping closer.

Great. There goes my quick escape! I wasn't sure which was worse, everyone thinking I was some sort of hero, or getting busted by the guards.

"I thought it might help Mac remember his home, that's all," I said.

"But how did you know to bring that specific car?" Howard asked.

"How did I know? Honestly, Howard, the car told me. First, it started to glow, then it spun a few laps around Mac's desk. It was kind of show-offy, actually."

Howard, Mom, Tabitha and Dennis stared at me. Apparently, they had no idea what to make of what I'd just said. Who could blame them? It didn't matter. I was done lying.

"All I can say to that is hallelujah and God bless!" Howard

smiled. "That particular car, Bertie, it has a story. It was the last gift Mac's mother bought him. It's not a grand story; they were just standing in a Target checkout line when Mac spotted the car. Some other kid had decided to not buy it. Anyway, Mac had to have that little car. Normally, Mac's mom, Sandra, wouldn't have given in. She had rules, strict rules, but on that day, she broke them. And Mac made a special place in his heart for that tiny three-dollar race car. A month later, Sandra … she passed on."

Howard kept smiling, but I could see it was more difficult for him. "Forgive me for rambling, Bertie. What I'm trying to say is … thank you."

"You're welcome," I said. My eyes flew wide. Neck Tattoo and Muscle Guy Guard were getting closer. Ten steps away from me. I had nowhere to run. Those guys were nearly on me like a flea infestation.

Five steps away from getting busted. What to do?

"Howard, can I give you a hug?" I said.

"Sure you can!" he said.

I jumped to Howard as Tabitha fumed and Mom beamed. Clinging to Howard's chest, I hid inside his hug. Neck Tattoo and Muscle Guy walked right past me.

29

Lighter Than Air

A puffed-up full moon was peeking over the treetops.

Leon chewed.

I paced.

We were inside Leon's kennel. My dog ate kibble as I gave him an angry Mac and Better Bertie and Mom and Morton gang update. Mom and Howard were spending the night at the hospital with Mac. Tabitha, the six remaining Morton relatives, and I were camping out at Howard's house.

And that's why I was angry.

Five minutes earlier, I was doing fine. I was in the pantry scooping dog food into Leon's bowl when I overhead a Morton aunt on her phone. I don't remember her name, but she had unnatural red hair, bad taste in shoes, and a big mouth. "Pathetic, pinning all their hopes on a toy car." Big

Mouth's tone turned into rattlesnake venom. "And that girl, the one who caused poor Mac's condition to begin with. Oh, I can't even look at her, I just can't. She makes me sick. Howard is a fool for taking them in."

When I left the hospital, I felt hopeful for Mac. I'm talking super-hopeful. And Big Mouth stole that feeling from me. Thief! The police should probably arrest her and toss her in jail.

Yeah, I could imagine Better Bertie saying I was "choosing to be angry." Too bad! A girl's got to blame somebody, right?

My lungs were knotted so tight it stung to breathe. While Leon chewed kibble, I paced, and finished giving him the update.

"Operation Monkey Butt is officially a go," I said. "By this time tomorrow, Dad will be here. We are going home, Leon."

Leon looked up at me and farted.

It was time for the glasses.

Sliding them on, I saw a bright light shine from the roof of the doghouse. Better Bertie stood atop it, glowing, radiant. In her hand was a small yellow card.

"What's that card you're holding?" I asked.

In a flash, Better Bertie vanished from the doghouse roof, then she reappeared on the other side of me. "It's for you."

Taking the card, I saw it was a *Get Out Of Jail Free* card

from Monopoly. I was pretty sure Better Bertie was shaming me for leaving the hospital. And, come tomorrow, for leaving Altoona with my father.

"Ha-ha!" I said. "Are you trying to make me even angrier?"

"No. You do an excellent job of that on your own."

"Yes, I do." It actually surprised me that I was agreeing with Better Bertie. My chest kept saying I needed help. I found it harder and harder to breathe. "Why do I do that? Why do I beat myself up?"

"Do you really want to know?" she asked.

"Oh, c'mon, man! Do you always have to answer my questions with another question? How can you be a better version of me when you're so annoying?"

"Do you really want to know?"

Before I could reply, Better Bertie laughed. "Sorry, girl, you can't tee me up like that." Putting on a more serious expression, she said, "Here's the deal. People beat themselves up because they don't know how to let go of things. Instead of letting stuff pass, they hold onto it. And sometimes, when it gets really bad, like what you've been doing for almost three years now, they hold on so tightly it hurts."

"So how do I let go of things?" I asked. "Do *not* say 'Do you really want to know?'"

She didn't.

Instead, Better Bertie told me to fetch a magic marker and some of the "*get well soon*" balloons that various visitors had left for Mac. She said to write down whatever I was mad at on the balloons. One problem: I had a lot of anger, and only three balloons. Those puppies filled up fast. I started writing tiny, and I still ran out of room. I needed a hundred balloons to get it all out of me.

I scanned some of the random things I had written.

"Mac's hurt so bad because of me."

"Big Mouth Aunt is a hope thief."

"Legalese Daddy."

"Stupid divorce."

"Mom is angry at me."

"Ruined Mom and Howard's relationship."

"Tabitha wants to smash my face."

"Miss my Carver City friends."

"Scared of what Sandra Morton's ghost wants from me."

"Marker fumes are giving me a headache."

Minutes later, I met Better Bertie on the roof of Howard's house. I clutched the balloon strings, feeling ridiculous.

Better Bertie motioned to the moonlit sky above us, while smiling like a glowing idiot. "Release the balloons," she said, waving her arms. "Let 'em go."

Here's the thing: I didn't want to let the strings go. I'm

not sure why, but I was hesitant. "This feels so dumb," I said. "Plus, I didn't have enough balloons."

"Girl, you don't need a few more balloons, you need a balloon factory! Now let go."

So I did it. I released the strings.

The balloons floated up.

My eyes followed the three balloons bearing my list of angry and fearful messages. They rose above the trees, toward the full moon. They drifted and danced higher and further away, moving in the same direction like migrating birds.

"What now?" I asked.

"You released your problems to a higher power," Better Bertie said. "How are you feeling?"

I told her the cold hard truth. "I don't know. I mean, I get that you want me to tell you that you were right and you're so smart and wonderful. But sorry, dude, it's not like I'm feeling anything new or better or different going on."

"You're not paying attention, Bertie. This isn't about gaining something, it's about losing something. Flip the script, and think about what you've lost."

A few deep breaths later, I began to laugh.

"Oh, you're good," I said. "You're really good!"

"Better believe it, baby girl." Better Bertie grinned. "Keep talking!"

"Well, you were right: I have lost something. The tightness in my chest is gone. I'm like seriously breathing easy. Wow, it feels good. Ha-ha. This is crazy!"

"No, Bertie. This is letting go."

It felt like a great weight had been lifted off me. I felt light. Lighter than air. Until …

"Who are you talking to, Froot Loops?"

Tabitha. Her head stuck out of an attic window. She posed another snarky question.

"And why are you on my roof, wearing sunglasses at night?"

Technically, she had posed three snarky questions. I had to admit, all of them were legit.

30

The Woman With Two Brown Thumbs

"If I told you who I was talking to and why I'm on your roof wearing sunglasses at night, you wouldn't believe me," I said, taking off the glasses.

My hope was Tabitha would just call me a weirdo or make some other mean comment about me seeing ghosts. I wanted her to go away.

Instead, she stepped out onto the roof.

"Where did you get those glasses?" she said. "I've seen them somewhere before."

My chest tightened. And I didn't have any balloons left to release.

"I found them in the hospital chapel. A … woman left them behind."

"And you didn't hand them into the Lost and Found?"

she asked. "Wow. You're a liar and a thief."

That was when I nearly told Tabitha that her mother had left the sunglasses for me because she wanted me to have them. But I stopped myself. Instead I said, "Can I ask you a strange question?"

Tabitha shrugged.

"Did your mother wear lavender perfume?" I said.

Tabitha looked at me like she wanted to push me off the roof. It was a long way down to the ground, so I braced myself.

"Who told you that?" she said. "My dad or my grandparents? Who?"

I shrugged. "Well, I've met a ton of Mortons…"

"And all of them hate your guts."

"So I've been told."

Walking carefully past Tabitha, I headed toward the open attic window.

"My mother didn't wear perfume." she said.

I stopped. Looked back.

"She loved flowers, but she had two brown thumbs." Tabitha said. "It's the truth. Whatever flowers my mom planted always died, except for lavender. So she grew that plant everywhere. She filled up half the backyard and part of the front yard with it."

Lost in memories, Tabitha's tone softened.

"When the moon was full like it is tonight, she would grab blankets and take Mac and me up here to the roof. Then she'd point to the yard, so happy. 'Look at the lavender, guys. In the moonlight, the purple and blue petals look like a sea of stars.'"

Glancing at the backyard below us, I saw something was happening. Something magical, fragrant, and Better Bertie-like. Thousands of brilliant lavender flowers grew in an instant. It took my breath in the best of ways.

Colored in twinkling moonlight, the flowers did look like a sea of stars. Because of Tabitha's silence, I knew the flower show could only be seen with my funky sunglasses.

"What happened to all the lavender flowers? Where'd they go?" I said.

"My dad pulled them out of the ground after my mom died," Tabitha said. "He's a rock with almost everything. No, he's a mountain. But the mountain started to crumble. He couldn't take it. They reminded him of Mom too much."

"Is that why there are no pictures of your mom in the house?"

"Stop it! Stop asking me questions like we are friends!"

I nodded. We said nothing for a few uncomfortable seconds.

"Tomorrow night, my dad's coming for me," I said.

"I know that already."

Her tone was spiteful again. "I heard my dad and your mom talking. Your father is worried that if Mac doesn't get better, we'll sue him for what you did. So he's taking you to North Carolina like it's your *Get Out of Jail Free* card or something."

"Or something," was all I could manage to say. How did Better Bertie know that Tabitha was going to mention a *Get Out of Jail Free* card? Another mystery waiting to be solved. They were piling up.

"Whatever. It's for the best," she said. "This way, we both get what we want."

Not really, I thought. The only thing I wanted was for Mac to be Mac again. Awake and happy, riding his bike around town while he kept an eye out for his missing dog, Cosmo.

"Tabitha Morton!" A familiar voice shouted behind us. Tabitha and I looked that way. Big Mouth Aunt was in the attic window. She shot me a hateful glare, and waved frantically to Tabitha.

"Come on, Tabby, we are going to the hospital. Hurry! It's *urgent*."

31

Hospital Personnel Only!

"Severe hypotensive crisis," Dr. Myles said, to a colleague in scrubs.

The brain surgeon barked orders to nurses and technicians as they rushed Mac's gurney to the operating room. "Fifty cc's of AD, stat. Boost his BP. Don't look at me, just do it!"

Mac was so incredibly pale. He looked more ghostly than human. And Dr. Myles had a sickly glow. He was afraid Mac was going to die. I watched dark nasty waves of fear radiate off him in red and green. A chill ran through me. The surgeon's fears affected everyone around him. Auras were blending together, deepening and darkening people's anxieties. Like a deadly virus, the fear was contagious.

Howard, Mom, and the Morton gang jogged behind Mac's gurney. They called out, "Hang in there, Mac" and

"You'll be fine in no time." Better Bertie and I followed a few steps behind. I almost slid off the glasses. Many people said encouraging things, but their aura colors said the exact opposite. In other words, they were lying.

Except for Tabitha. It seemed like she was the only one who truly believed that her brother would get better.

"Fight, Mac!" she yelled. "You beat me in arm wrestling last week, remember?" She was trying to will her brother well. "Fight like that now! Be strong!"

Mac's left hand flopped over, and his little red race car clattered to the floor. Everyone following the gurney was so focused on Mac that nobody noticed.

Vroom. Coming to life, the Hot Wheels car navigated through the onslaught of stomping feet, right to my sneakers. *Vroom-vroom!* I was super-scared for Mac and didn't feel like smiling. But the little car gave me hope. I snatched it up.

Automatic doors leading to the operating room hall opened. Nurses, doctors, and orderlies rushed Mac inside, and the doors shut behind them.

Ginger-bearded Orderly Dude gestured to a sign. *HOSPITAL PERSONNEL ONLY.*

"Think I care about your stupid sign? That's my son," Howard said. "Step aside and let me in!" The orderly didn't budge. I truly thought Howard was gonna slug the orderly right in the chops. Hot blue and red charges of electricity crackled off Howard's head like angry lightning bolts. The colors of chaos, fear, and rage.

Big Mouth Aunt pulled Howard away and told him to calm down. Howard looked like was going to slug her, too. I definitely wanted to hit her. Her aura was the colors of contempt, judgment, and suckiness.

Howard, Mom, and the Morton relatives bickered amongst themselves. Everyone had an opinion about how Mac's situation should be handled. They were daytime talk show crazy. And yet, holding the red race car Mac loved so much … Well, it made me feel calm. For once, I was the only peaceful person in the vicinity.

Saying a quick "see you as soon as I can" to Better Bertie, I slipped off my glasses. It was 1:30 in the morning, and I didn't want to draw more mean looks. I approached Ginger-bearded Orderly Dude.

"Excuse me. I know this will sound really strange, but Mac's going to need this race car." The orderly gave me a funny look as I held the race car out for him to take. "Told you, right? Anyway, it's like a lifeline for him. I and all the angry people behind me would be forever in your debt if you could get it to him as soon as possible."

Still acting like it was an odd request, Ginger-bearded

Orderly Dude nodded. "Okay, kid. Will do."

"Can you maybe promise you'll do it?" I said. "Sorry, but I'd feel a lot better if you promised. Your 'will do' didn't have a ton of oomph. And Mac, he's the only Morton alive who can stand the sight of my face, so we need him alive and kicking."

"Okay, I promise." He took the car and said, "Now go away."

Smiling gratefully, I turned on my heel. My glasses plopped down onto my face. I jumped halfway out of my body. I was nose-to-nose with Sandra Morton's ghost. She hovered three feet above the floor tiles. Her long, blond-white hair and blood red dress undulated as if she were floating underwater. The water must have been freezing because Sandra Morton gave off a distinct chill. My skin went numb, and my veins felt like they were filled with crushed ice. It was painful. I shivered head-to-toe. Looking into Sandra's eyes, I saw them turning black and shiny and more terrifying than anything I'd ever seen. Dark veins and arteries shifted underneath her transparent skin. I just stood there stupidly, wide-eyed, open-mouthed, shaking all over, and certain this ghost was going to kill me for what I had done to her beloved son.

"Hello, Bernice."

I opened my mouth to scream, but nothing came out.

"My son is dying as we speak, and I need to go see him," the ghost said.

Since I couldn't scream, I ran.

Sandra Morton called to me, a warning. "I'll be coming back for you soon. *Very* soon. You can't hide from a ghost, Bernice."

I glanced back and saw Sandra Morton pass through the *HOSPITAL PERSONNEL ONLY* sign on the operating room door, vapor style.

32

Tell Him Now

Dr. Myles finished Mac's emergency surgery around dawn. His prognosis for Mac was "wait and see."

Everyone had been up all night, hoping and praying for good news.

The Morton gang staked claim to the waiting room. The assault of icy looks was too much for me to take, so I told Mom I'd be hanging out in the snack machine room. I think she wanted to come with me, but I knew Howard needed her more than I did. What Mom didn't know was that I had Better Bertie to keep me company.

For hours, Better Bertie and I prayed for Mac. I kept expecting Sandra Morton to come haunt me, torture me, or do something vengeful and ghosty. But nothing like that happened.

Better Bertie said, "I like Sandra's aggressive style. The fear of fear is often more crippling than the fear itself."

"Thanks for that little pearl of wisdom," I said as I took off the sunglasses. "Did you get it from a teabag?"

It was time for a Better Bertie break. At that moment, I didn't want any advice. I didn't even want to be a better person. I just wanted to ... be.

Anyway, despite all my pent-up anxiety for Mac and for me, I somehow drifted off to sleep with my head on the table. It must've been a deep-deep sleep.

When I woke up, I was horrified to see two things.

One: I had drooled all over the table.

Two: Howard was holding my sunglasses.

"Knew it! Barnard Optical," Howard said, reading the company name on my shades.

"Any change with Mac?" I asked.

Howard shook his head.

"Barnard Optical went belly-up after customers complained that the lenses of their sunglasses caused odd visual distortions," he said. "The company was sued into oblivion."

"What kind of distortions?" I asked.

"Double vision, flashing lights, mirror imaging. In the optometrist trade, we call them 'ghost trails.' The manufacturer screwed up the chemical composite for reactive shading. I

148

had to buy back every pair I sold. Only one person refused to return them, my late wife." He paused, remembering. "She said the sunglasses helped her see the world in a new way, and when she looked closely enough, she saw beauty everywhere. Even if things looked terrifying at first, they could still have ripples of beauty."

Howard handed me my sunglasses and gave me a curious look that almost seemed like an accusation, like maybe he thought I had stolen them. "So where did you find these glasses? Back at the house?"

"The hospital chapel." I slid them on and nearly fell out of my chair.

"Ah!" I screamed. The ghost of Sandra Morton hovered above me all shimmery and spooky-like.

Startled by my scream, Howard spilled his coffee and shot me an exhausted look. "What now?" he asked.

Before I could answer, Sandra Morton said, "Tell Howard I'm here, Bernice."

I couldn't tell him that. He'd freak out on me. But what could I say that would not cause Howard to blow a fuse?

Gesturing to the glasses, I said, "You're right about the lenses, Howard. Been seeing ghost trails."

His phone rang. Hurrying out of the room, he took the call.

149

"Bad girl, Bernice. You should've listened to me!" Sandra Morton warned.

"He wouldn't have believed me," I said. "I don't hardly believe me!"

"Nobody believes you, kid!" At the door, I heard a sarcastic sigh. Big Mouth Aunt and Uncle Dennis came in. Big Mouth shot me a *you're nuttier than squirrel droppings* look and sat at my table. Basically, she was telling me to scram. And I was more than happy to do that. Racing out into the hallway, I heard Big Mouth shrieking. "Ew! Is this drool? I put my hand in it!"

I continued sprinting for an exit, but here's a spooky fact: you can't outrun a ghost. Sandra Morton appeared out of thin air before me.

"Going somewhere, Bernice?"

"Please leave me alone. And stop calling me Bernice!" I said.

"No! You and I, we've got work to do."

"What do you want from me?

"You're about to find out."

"But I can't do anything. I'm just a kid."

"So is Mac."

Gusting winds swirled. I gasped in shock. Sandra Morton's face turned darker and more sinister, misshapen like melting wax.

She pointed a crooked finger to Room 555.

The door flew open on its own. This time, the room wasn't empty. Howard was inside, dialing his cell.

"Tell him, Bernice," Sandra Morton said. "Tell Howard I'm here!"

"I told you, he won't believe me."

Howard glanced up from his phone.

"I won't believe what, Bertie? Who are you talking to?"

"Tell him now!" Sandra roared.

Here goes nothing.

"Howard, I'm talking to the ghost of your dead wife," I said. "And she's not happy."

Clang.

He dropped his phone

33

Howard's Surprise

"Whatever twisted game you are playing, young lady, you've gone too far," Howard was furious. "For your mother's sake, I promised myself I'd give you the benefit of the doubt. I swore I wouldn't lose my temper. Well, guess what? I'm losing it!"

"Howard, I'm sorry," I said. "But your first wife is hovering beside you!"

The angry electrical charges I had seen earlier in Howard's aura returned.

"Stop it, Bertie!" Bending down, he grabbed his cell and saw that the screen was cracked. Howard's lightning bolt aura flashed a deeper red, like he wanted to smash me. He started for the door. But Sandra Morton's ghost wasn't done with me.

"Ask if him he's still a terrible singer, Bertie." Ghost

152

Sandra saw me hesitate. Her ghoulish features intensified. "DO IT!"

"Your wife wants to know if you're still a terrible singer," I said, looking away from the creepy ghost.

Howard slowed momentarily, as if caught off guard. But he was so mad, he wouldn't let himself stop. "Don't talk to me! Haven't you done enough, Bernice?"

Now it gets really strange.

Sandra's ghost floated inside me.

Inside me!

My body went cold. I smelled lavender. I felt love. A mother's love. A wife's love. And then I started singing. Or, more precisely, *we* started singing. *"Ooh-ooh child, things are gonna get easier. Ooh-ooh child, things'll get brighter."*

Howard stopped. Turned around in shock. "Who told you to sing that song?"

The Bertie-Sandra Morton Ghost duet didn't answer, we just sang louder. *"Some day, yeah, we'll put it together and we'll get it all done."* It wasn't simply strange having a ghost take over my body; it was magnificently strange.

What Sandra was up to, I had no idea. But nothing about it felt dark or sinister. More than anything it felt bittersweet. Hopeful and helpless and a little bit desperate, all at the same time. For our big finish, we did a quick dance spin. *"Some*

day, yeah, we'll walk in the rays of a beautiful sun!"

Tears filled the astonished optometrist's eyes, and all the raging red electrical charges surrounding him dissolved away. "How … how can this be?"

WHOOSH!

Sandra's ghost floated out of me. As she left, my strength left me, too. My legs caved. I fell, but Howard caught me before I hit the floor. My body felt like I'd run a marathon at a full sprint. Peering up to Sandra, I saw she was beautiful and lovely and luminous once again.

"Forgive me, Bernice," she said. "It's a side effect following a ghostly occupation. I'm not quite right, either."

"Oh, goodie." I sighed. "Please stop calling me Bernice."

"Are you talking to Sandra?" Howard asked. "What's she saying, Bertie? Does she have a message for me?"

"Need a minute, Howard. I just got body-snatched!"

He helped me stand up.

Sandra hovered, looking down at me. Not to get all new-agey, but it was like she was looking into my soul. Sandra was a ghost mother on a mission.

A speeding swirl of words formed in my brain.

Sandra's words.

They shot out from my mouth. "Sandra does have a message for you …"

More words flew out.

"She says you have to stop, Howard. She says you're hurting Mac."

Howard didn't like that.

"Me? Hurting Mac? Sandra would never say that!"

"You believe Mac is going to die, Howard," I said, with the ghost's help. "You believe it, and Mac knows you believe it. So why should he keep fighting?"

Howard's aura dulled into the lifeless color of doom. Sandra must've spoken the truth.

34

The Mind Meld

"**H**is condition just gets worse and worse." Howard made a heartfelt confession. "I keep fighting my fears and doubts, but I'm losing—I'm losing hope. Losing faith. I guess I haven't been hiding it as well as I thought."

"Not to Mac. That's the reason Sandra is using me to reach out to you," I said, channeling Sandra's words. "Mac feels your energy and senses your thoughts, Howard, even in a coma. You're not just his dad, you're his hero. And if his hero loses all hope, Mac will, too."

Howard hung his head in anguish. His colors were icky, a disturbing mix of guilt and shame and hopelessness.

Ghost Mom kept giving me words to share with her former husband.

"Sandra says this isn't Mac's time to die, Howard, that he's stuck between worlds. Mac needs things that anchor him to Altoona or he won't be able to come back. Even little things like the Hot Wheels race car could help him find his way home. You saw it firsthand, how he gripped that little car with a strength he should not have."

"But how do I help Mac?" Howard said. "If Mac is sensing how lost I am, how can I avoid making things even worse?"

I felt Sandra's response in my head. I shook my head *no*. Making a timeout sign with my hands, I looked at Ghost Mom floating above. "Really sorry, Mrs. Morton, but those words, they don't work for me. C'mon, you're calling Howard 'my love,' and stuff, and it's just like *ick*."

In an instant, Sandra Morton's ghost sent me different words.

"Ah, much better," I said. "Thank you, that will work."

I looked at Howard and said, "Sandra says you have to find your hope again."

That made him angry.

"You think I haven't been trying?" Howard tapped his chest with his hand. "It's as if I have nothing left in me! And now Mac is running out of time. Tell Sandra I can't do this alone."

More of Sandra's words popped into my head.

"Sandra knows you can't do it alone, Howard," I said. "That's why she's bringing someone here to help you."

"Who?" he said. "Who's going to help?"

I waited for the answer to appear. Sandra sent me no words to relay. We stood in silence. Or actually, one of us hovered ghost-style.

"Who is Sandra sending to help me?" Howard repeated.

Sandra Morton's ghost didn't need to answer his question. The answer literally walked into the room.

"What are you guys doing in here?" A familiar, soft, and beautiful voice said. Howard, Sandra Morton, and I looked to the doorway.

It was my mom.

"Everything okay?" she asked.

"Ah, yes," Howard said. He fumbled through his thoughts. "Bertie and I were just discussing … the unique history of her sunglasses. A few years ago, I sold that particular brand in my practice. Anyway, Bertie she's … quite a unique young lady."

Huh?

Mom clearly wasn't sure what to make of that statement. It could mean a whole lot of things. She gave me a quick look for reassurance that I hadn't caused another Morton catastrophe. I gave her a thumbs up. Looking at Howard,

Mom said, "Well, alright then. I'm heading down to the chapel. Thought I'd say a prayer for Mac."

Sandra Morton's ghost smiled.

I did, too.

"Can I join you?" Howard said.

"Always." Mom smiled.

Finally, Howard smiled. And you know what? It was a hopeful smile.

Howard and Mom headed off to the chapel, hand-in-hand.

For a moment, I thought about what I just witnessed. It blew me away. The grace and generosity of what Sandra's ghost had just done. Check it out: Sandra Morton used her ghostly influence to send my mom to help Howard, the love of Sandra's former life. Sandra did this in the hopes that Howard would find enough faith to help Mac wake from his coma. And Mac was in that coma because of me. All those twisty connections added up to one thing. Sandra Morton was the coolest ghost alive!

Or undead? Or actually dead?

"Mrs. Morton, can I ask you a question?"

"Call me Sandra, and I will call you Bertie. Deal?"

"Deal," I said.

"What's your question, Bertie?"

"I'm just kind of wondering what it's like for you. I mean, is it scary being dead? Where do you go when you die? And when you get there, what do you do?"

"That's three questions."

"Three awesome questions!"

"More like *big* questions. And I can only give you little answers and hope they make sense." She lowered herself so we were nearly eye-to-eye, "Don't be afraid, Bertie. The afterlife isn't scary. In fact, it's more magnificent than any words could ever say. After I died, I went to an afterworld way station of sorts, a place where souls get ready to move on. The way station is where you learn to let go of the life you knew on Earth. People, places, everything. It's where you learn to love without the pain."

"So you don't miss living in Altoona?" I said.

"No, I don't. I've learned to let Altoona go."

"What about Howard and Tabitha and Mac? You don't miss them, either?"

"I miss them so much it hurts." The ghost mom forced herself to smile.

My heart broke for her. The pain she felt. The sacrifice she was making,

"Sandra, I'm sorry," I said. "And I swear if I could change what I did, how I hurt Mac, I would—"

"Stop! Don't finish that sentence. Feeling guilty won't help Mac or you or anyone else. If you want to change things, Bertie, change how you live your one precious life from this moment on."

"But there's nothing more I can do for Mac. Plus, I'll be leaving town soon." I motioned to a clock on the wall. "My father will be here in a couple of hours to take me home to North Carolina."

Before Sandra could respond, we heard a horrific wail, followed by four terrible words shouted by a frantic nurse. "Code Blue, Room 548!"

35

Any Moment Now

For the second time in twenty-four hours, Mac went into cardiac arrest.

A rush of doctors and nurses managed to revive him, but Mac's condition was now beyond critical. *Grave* is the word Dr. Myles used, which basically meant it was just about time to start digging one of those awful things at the nearest cemetery. No matter what anyone did, all the prayers we prayed, that amazing eight-year-old boy was getting worse every minute.

When things quieted down a bit, I went to Mac's door and peeked through a window with my glasses. It was stunning how much was going on, most of which no one else but me could see.

Ginger-bearded Orderly Dude had kept his promise.

Mac had the magical Hot Wheels race car in his left hand. The brave little car was trying its best to vroom-vroom, but it just didn't have enough power. Its engine and headlights sputtered, like Dad's old Corvette used to do when the battery wouldn't hold a charge.

Tabitha sat at Mac's bedside holding his right hand and praying, and talking to her brother.

It wasn't enough.

Sandra hovered over Mac's bed. She touched her baby boy's face with her ghostly hands, sending him her mother's love from The Great Beyond.

Even that wasn't enough. It was like Mac had lost his will to live.

In the hall, Dr. Myles spoke to Howard and Mom in a whisper. He told them there was nothing medical the hospital staff could do for Mac. On an iPad, the doctor showed Howard and my mom Mac's latest EEG readout. Mac's brain wave lines should've been a bunch of peaks and valleys, but instead they were nearly all straight lines and only a few little bumps. Mac's brain activity had all but stopped.

"Howard, you need to prepare yourself for what's coming," Dr. Myles said. "Mac doesn't have long. He could leave us at any moment, I'm afraid."

"Well, I'm not afraid," Howard said, shaking his head

defiantly. "And I don't give a damn what you think, Dr. Carson, or what the EEG says, either. My son will find his way back. I'm NOT giving up on him!"

Through my glasses I saw Howard's aura—it was bright, and angry. He wasn't lying to the surgeon. He truly believed that Mac would wake up and heal. He squeezed Mom's hand for support. She was now Howard's lifeline.

Sandra's ghost suddenly appeared. She turned to me with a fierce look. A ferocious mother bear protecting her cubs kind of gaze.

"I need you to go somewhere, Bertie," she said. "This instant!"

36

Mystery Mission

The Morton relatives filled the hallway. They were scared, worried, and frustrated, and they wanted someone to blame for Mac's poor health. I was that someone.

Stepping away from Mac's room, I tried to navigate through the collection of dirty looks. Grabbing the strap of my backpack, Big Mouth Aunt spun me around. "Just because your lawyer daddy is coming to pick you up, doesn't mean that this is over. If Mac doesn't make it, so help me, I'll make it my life's mission …" Stopping mid-sentence, Big Mouth Aunt screamed as if she had seen a ghost. "Ack!"

No, she hadn't seen a ghost, she had felt one. I spotted Sandra's ghost body sliding out of Big Mouth Aunt's body after a brief occupation.

"Awful-awful woman. And such a bore," Sandra said.

165

Floating ahead of the Morton gang, Mac's ghost mom said, "Hurry, Bertie. Snack room. We don't have much time."

The Morton relatives parted like the Red Sea, and I ran to meet Sandra. In the snack room, she floated down to my eye level.

"Earlier, you said you wanted to help Mac. Are you ready to do that?"

"Of course," I said. "Whatever I can do!"

"Good, because I'm sending you on a mission."

"What kind of mission?"

"Don't talk, just listen. In nine minutes, a purple Subaru will pull up in front of the hospital. The driver will power down the window and ask for Tabitha Morton. You and Tabitha will get inside the Subaru, and it will take you where I need you to go."

"Whoa-whoa. Did you say me and Tabitha?"

"Yes. And I also said don't talk, just listen."

"But Tabitha isn't gonna go anywhere with me."

"Not unless you convince her."

"Convince her to do what? I don't even know what we're talking about, Sandra. But I do know I can't convince your daughter of anything. She hates me."

"Bertie, I don't have time to explain all that's happening. The gears of the universe are turning as we speak. Now, I have

166

to get back to Mac, and you've got to do what I'm telling you to do, or Mac will die. Do you understand, Bertie? Tell me you understand!"

"I don't understand."

"Good, let's go with that. In fifty-five seconds, Tabitha will walk into this room and put quarters into the soda machine for a ginger ale, but she will be a quarter shy. She'll be irritated. You have some change in your left pocket, so give her a quarter. From there you are on your own. Eight minutes, purple Subaru. Good luck, got to go!"

Before I could object, Sandra whisked through the wall and vanished.

A moment later, Sandra's ghost head popped back in and said, "One last thing. Don't forget to buy the cookies, okay?"

I said, "Cookies? What cookies?"

But Sandra was gone.

"Okay, fine, cookies, whatever," I muttered, shaking my head.

That was when Tabitha walked in.

We locked eyes for a moment, but Tabitha didn't say a word. Turning to the soda machine, she pumped quarters into the slot. She huffed, irritated. She was one quarter shy of buying a ginger ale.

37

I Know I Sound Crazy

Pulling a quarter from my left pocket, I was about to give it to Tabitha. Bad idea, I quickly realized. She wouldn't take it from me, I could tell from the icy look on her face. Instead, I pushed it into the soda machine and pressed the ginger ale button.

Ka-thump.

The green can landed at the bottom of the chute.

When I walked away, I felt Tabitha staring at me, even more irritated. The clock was ticking, and my chances of convincing her to come with me on a mystery mission was stuck on zero. Pulling a notebook from my backpack, I jotted down a note as fast as I could.

"If this soda is for me, I don't want ginger ale." Tabitha said.

"Yes you do."

168

"Oh, yeah? How do you know that?"

Ripping out the notebook page, I folded it just so.

"I said how do you know that, Bernice?"

I handed the note to Tabitha. She unfolded it and read it.

I know I sound crazy, but even crazy people sometimes know what's most important. Want to help Mac? Follow me.

I left the snack room, hoping Tabitha would take the bait and give chase.

38

Cookies

The hospital's front doors opened. The note worked. I had needed Tabitha to meet me outside, and there she was.

She stalked toward me, eyes narrowed, ready for a fight. "Why did you give this to me?" Holding up my note, Tabitha said, "If this is some kind of sick joke ..."

"I promise, it's no joke," I said.

"You think you know something that can help save Mac?" she said. "Okay, fine! What is it? Tell me."

"Well, I don't actually know yet. But in another minute, I will."

Tabitha scowled. She probably wanted to whack me. Everything in her aura was saying *I'm gonna snap you in two.* My brain told me to wave my hands around martial arts style to deflect incoming punches. Since I had zero martial arts training, that probably made me look even more cuckoo's nest crazy.

"Just hear me out, Tabitha, okay? In a few minutes a purple Subaru will appear. The woman driving will power down her window and ask for Tabitha Morton. You and I are supposed to get in."

"To go where?" Tabitha said. "And how's that supposed to help Mac?"

"I don't know the answer to either of those questions yet," I said. "Oh wait. We are supposed to buy cookies, too."

"Cookies?" Tabitha lost it. "Have you gone *full* Froot Loops?"

"This isn't what you think, Tabitha. I just want to help Mac."

"Know what I think? I think I want to punch you in the face. But you'll be gone in another hour, and I won't have to see your ugly lying face ever again. You're an awful girl, *Bernice.* Go back to North Carolina and leave me and my family alone." She stormed to the doors.

It was an impossible situation, a genuine "now or never" moment. I didn't want to say it, but I had to say it. "Tabitha, your mom said you have to come with me."

Tabitha stopped cold. Stalking back, she glared at me. "My mom?"

171

"I know I sound crazy, I really do. That's why I wrote it on the note. I'm sorry, Tabitha. But the truth is I can see and talk to your mom's ghost. And she told me that Mac's life depends on you and me getting inside that purple Subaru."

By now, Tabitha likely didn't just want to punch me in the face, she wanted to kick my teeth out, too. And I was going to let her. I needed her help so bad, I had to accept the punches and kicks, and whatever else she threw at me. I didn't even do my stupid martial arts thing.

Only Tabitha didn't punch me or kick me. Instead, she pinned me against a brick wall. My head conked a NO ANIMALS ALLOWED sign, and I saw stars. My glasses fell askew. One of my eyes saw Tabitha in the human world, and my other eye saw her in the spirit world. Strangely, this made me feel bad for her. Tabitha wasn't just furious anymore. She was hurt, too. And confused.

"You're not only awful, Bernice Blount, you're evil!" she said. "Why do you want to hurt us?" Tearing up, she spoke through gritted teeth. "What did my family ever do to you?"

"Tabitha Morton!" A female voice called.

Looking over her shoulder, Tabitha saw a woman smiling from the open window of a purple Subaru. "Are you Tabitha? I'm Miko, your Uber driver. Ready to roll?"

Tabitha glanced at me, suspicious. "You set this up?"

172

I shook my head. "No, I swear. I don't even have an Uber account."

"Neither do I," Tabitha said.

Popping out of the car, Miko told Tabitha to check her confirmation code.

Tabitha pulled out her phone and saw there was indeed a confirmation message. "I don't get it. According to this, I called for a ride twelve minutes ago."

"Tabitha, your mom told me this would happen," I said. "Just like she told me you would be a quarter short when you tried to buy a can of ginger ale in the snack room."

A struggle played out on Tabitha's face. It was like her good wolf wanted to trust me, and her bad wolf wanted to punch me.

"We have to take this Uber," I said. "For Mac."

Miko smiled. "Give me a second here, guys, I have to move some boxes." She swung open the back door of her car so Tabitha and I could see something. I shouldn't have been shocked, but I was.

"I sell them on the side for my daughter." Miko said. "Got a sweet tooth, girls?"

Tabitha's jaw dropped, and then her eyes widened. Stacked in Miko's backseat were four cases of Girl Scout cookies.

We were taking that Uber.

39

The Hat

During the ride, I bought us each a box of cookies. Tabitha went with Thin Mints, and I got Savannah Smiles. We didn't know if we were supposed to eat them or not. Neither of us felt particularly hungry. Not to mention that there were a number of mysteries that had yet to be solved. For example, the mystery of where exactly we were going.

On the dashboard, Miko's GPS screen displayed 831 Hickory Avenue.

"Hickory's my street, but that isn't my house number," Tabitha said. "Why would my mother send us to that address?"

I shrugged my shoulders. "I don't know, but we'll find out soon enough."

Tabitha gave me a hard stare. She must've had a thousand questions, most of which I could not answer. "You're sure this is real? You talked to my mom?"

I nodded. "I wouldn't lie to you. Not about this."

"Well, what did she tell you?"

"Everything," I said. "Look, it's hard to describe, but your mom put thoughts into my mind, *her thoughts*, and they told me things."

"Like what things?"

"Like her nickname for you was 'Petal,' as in flower petal."

Tabitha softened ever so slightly. "Mac could've told you that before his accident."

"And your mom heard your prayers," I said. "All of them."

Tabitha's stricken face told me she wanted to believe me. She wanted this to be true. But she simply couldn't convince herself. Tabitha's two wolves were still battling.

"She wants you to know it wasn't the hat thing that caused her to get sick," I said.

Tabitha's eyes narrowed. "The hat thing?"

"You and your mom were going ice skating on Lake Mansel, and she told you to wear a hat, but you wouldn't do it. You guys argued, a big fight. Later, when your ears were freezing at the lake, your mom gave you her hat to wear. The next week, she was sick. Her cancer had come back. And ever since then, you've secretly thought it was because she gave you her hat."

Nodding, Tabitha's voice cracked, "My friends were skating. I wanted to look cool. I was so stupid." Hands flying to her face in shame, Tabitha tried not to cry, but there was no stopping it. Tears fell onto the tips of her fingers.

"Listen to me, okay? Your mom wants you to know it wasn't the hat. It had nothing to do with her getting sick, Tabitha. She's never been more proud of you, watching the brave girl you have become. And she will always-always love her Petal."

Reaching out, Tabitha took my hand in hers.

Through my sunglasses I saw her aura changing. Warm, inviting colors of relief and gratitude overtook harsh streaks of shame and pain. There was a beauty to the process. It reminded me of a time-lapse YouTube video of flowers blooming in fast motion.

For that moment, Tabitha's good wolf had won.

But someone else in the Subaru was crying, too.

"Almost there," Miko said.

Our Uber driver glanced at us with streaks of black mascara running down her face that made her look totally racoony. She blubbered, "Oh my God, I got to tell you guys, the hat story, it got me right here." She pointed to her heart. "I'm crushed!"

Through Miko's windshield I spotted a dog in the road.

176

I gasped in horror.

It wasn't just any dog.

It was Leon!

Miko was about to crush my dog.

I shouted, "LOOK OUT!"

40

831 Hickory

Miko and Tabitha and I screamed.

Brakes slammed.

Tires bit the road.

Birds flew from the trees.

Did we hit Leon? Everyone flew into a panic. Heart pounding, I opened my door. All three of us jumped out of the Uber. Scrambling to the front of Miko's car, we sighed in unison. Leon's nose was six inches from Miko's purple bumper. My beloved, farty dog was perfectly fine. Looking up at me with big brown eyes, he smiled and wagged his tail.

I picked Leon up and nuzzled him. "Thank you, God." Through my sunglasses, I saw joy and relief. Not on Leon, but on Miko and Tabitha. The three of us radiated happy colors as we cooed over Leon.

"What a little outlaw," I said, giving Leon a good scratch. "How'd you bust out of your kennel?"

Miko said, "My sweet girls, I feel so guilty for nearly running over your dog. Please take more boxes of cookies. It'll be on me, no charge. It's the least I can do."

I said, "You don't have to do that, Leon is fine. But, if you insist, I will gladly take two boxes of S'mores, thank you."

Meanwhile, the GPS voice in Miko's car kept announcing: "831 Hickory Avenue. You have arrived at your destination."

"Is this just a coincidence?" Tabitha whispered to me. "Leon somehow breaks out of his kennel, and ends up where my mother sent us at the exact same time."

"Wait," I said, eyes narrowing. "Where *did* she send us?"

"Good question," Tabitha said.

We turned.

Our eyes widened.

We gasped in horror.

We had been here before.

This was the last place we wanted to be.

831 Hickory Avenue was the home of Creepy Axe Murderer Guy. Ghost Mom had dispatched her daughter and me to the spookiest address in Altoona.

41

Enter And Die

"Why would my mom send us here?" Tabitha asked. "It makes zero sense."

Miko had just driven off in her Subaru. As we stood across from the axeman's house, Tabitha stowed four boxes of Girl Scout cookies in my backpack. I held Leon.

For once, luck was on our side: Creepy Axe Murderer Guy didn't appear to be at home. His driveway was empty. The biggest problem was Tabitha. She kept firing one question after another at me in full investigative reporter mode.

"Why didn't my mom tell us where we were going?"

"Are you sure you remember every single thing she told you to do?"

"How does us being here help Mac?"

"Will you *please* shut up?" I said.

"Excuse me?" Tabitha huffed.

"I said please, didn't I? I can't hardly think with you blasting me with questions."

"Too bad, because I have another one for you," she said. "How come you get to see my mom and not me, huh? It's not fair! She's *my* mother!"

Tabitha was right, it wasn't fair. But it was just another question I couldn't answer. When all the ghost stuff started, I'd figured it was the sunglasses. But then I remembered seeing Sandra Morton's ghost before I even had the glasses, so I still didn't know what was what. I kept wishing I could talk to Better Bertie, but she wasn't showing up anymore, and I felt lost without her. She's not just a better me, she's a *much* better me, and I needed her now.

So I decided to imagine what Better Bertie would do.

"Tell me what you see," I said, handing my sunglasses to Tabitha.

"Is it the glasses? Is that how you see ghosts?" she asked, sliding them on. She glanced about, hopeful. "What am I supposed to see? Am I looking for my mom, or what? All I see is a locked-up fence, a bunch of rusty junk, and some overgrown grass."

"Look at me," I said. "Do I have colors surrounding me, like an aura?"

"No. You look normal. Which is to say you look totally annoying."

"Give me my glasses."

Reluctantly, Tabitha handed me the glasses. Her face showed disappointment. We both had hoped the glasses would allow her to see her mother. And though I knew Sandra Morton's sunglasses helped me see what others couldn't see, now I was pretty sure there was something more to the equation.

Something in my blood.

My great-aunt Tillie had *vision*, or what she called "an extra eyeball" that allowed her to see what other people couldn't see. "A curse that sometimes disguised itself as a blessing," she'd told me, and vice-versa. And she said this: "If you want to break bread with angels, Bertie Bee, you better keep an extra chair at the table in case the devil shows up, looking for a free meal."

But I couldn't think about all that stuff now. I needed to focus. I put on the sunglasses and looked around. Everything I saw told me to run for my life.

Think of the worst nightmare you ever had. Now triple that, multiply it by a thousand, then add ten heaping scoops of the most demented horror movie misery you could ever imagine on top of it all. Creepy Axe Murderer Guy's house was so vile it stung my eyes to look at it. My heartbeat spiked in my ears. My throat closed so tightly I could barely breathe.

Here's the thing. The property had its own aura, and it looked like death.

A menacing black sandstorm of energy churned around the perimeter. Dark tendrils of hate twisted from the edges like hairy spider legs. Fierce red lightning bolts of rage sizzled a warning to one and all: *ENTER AND DIE!*

Feeling my fear, Leon growled.

"What's wrong, Bertie?" Tabitha said, alarmed. "Are you seeing something?"

"Yes, but I … can't really describe it."

"Since when has that stopped you?"

I opened my mouth to speak, but I still couldn't find the words.

"Bertie, tell me what you see!" Tabitha insisted.

"I see evil," I said.

Ripping the sunglasses from my face, I rubbed my aching eyes and caught my breath. "This is bad, Tabitha. Whoever this guy is, there's something really wicked here. I mean, no way he's your normal neighborhood creepster."

"Well, duh," Tabitha nodded. "His name is Jack Peak. People say he murdered two burglars who tried to rob his house like twenty years ago. Supposedly, he chopped them up and buried them in his backyard. I thought it was just an urban legend or something."

Hearing an oncoming rumble, I pushed Tabitha behind an elm tree.

Five seconds later, a junky Dodge truck rolled toward us.

Jack Peak had come home.

42

Climb the Oak

He parked his truck behind his house and lumbered to the open front gate like an angry giant. His aura was so dark and sinister, I briefly closed my eyes to get rid of it.

Tabitha, Leon, and I hid behind the elm tree.

Jack Peak glanced about with flaming lava eyes as he shut the gate. When he trudged inside his house, I whispered to Tabitha, "Hold Leon for me."

Taking him, she said, "Wait, Bertie. What are you doing?"

I didn't have time to answer. Running to a huge oak tree near Mr. Peak's fence, I ducked down and spied on the axeman. I saw him open a broken refrigerator in the backyard. Inside it was some sort of contraption with a big metal pot and steel tubing. Pulling out a mason jar of clear liquid, he drank it and grimaced.

Thump.

Someone grabbed my shoulder from behind. I almost literally died.

Spinning round, I saw it was Tabitha. She held Leon. Trying to calm my racing heart, I glared at Tabitha and whispered, "Don't ever sneak up on me!"

"Well don't just leave me behind then," she said. "My mom said we're supposed to do this together, remember?"

I couldn't argue with that.

"So we are here now. What are we going to do?" she asked.

Before I could say "I don't know" for the millionth time, my cell pinged. Looking down at my screen I saw a text. I read it, then I pointed to the twisted tree beside us. "We climb the oak."

"What are you talking about?" Tabitha said.

"The text I just got says '*climb the oak*'." I held up my screen as proof.

"There's nothing on your screen." Tabitha pointed. "Look."

I looked again. The text was still there. For my eyes, anyway.

"You don't see it?" I said. "Tabitha, this text is from your mom."

She swallowed a shaky breath. "Unbelievable! Something else I can't see."

Ping.

Another text from The Great Beyond. Tabitha and I swapped a look.

"Go ahead, Bertie," she said. "Tell me what it says."

"It says '*Hurry. Be brave. Climb the tree. You won't fall this time, Petal.*'"

Tabitha exhaled an OMG gasp. "It *is* from my mom." Tears spilled onto her face. "When I was eight, I fell out of a tree and broke my left arm."

Leon nuzzled her. I wanted to comfort Tabitha, but we had no time to be warm and fuzzy. Mac's life was at stake, and we had a tree to climb.

43

Texts From The Great Beyond

Leon didn't look up at Tabitha and me as we climbed the tree. All of his focus was on chewing a hunk of tree bark like it was a delicious bone.

He's kind of a weird dog.

Strange winds blew loud and strong. They pushed and pulled the oak tree's limbs as Tabitha and I climbed higher. Hands trembling, we clutched a long limb extending over Peak's backyard. One wrong move and we'd fall onto his fence spiked with rusty barbed wire.

From our vantage point we could survey nearly all of Peak's property. There was his parked truck, a couple half-collapsed sheds, piles of old junk everywhere, and two tall mounds of shoveled dirt. I sure hoped I wasn't gazing at our future graves.

Ping.

Another supernatural text. I checked my cell. The blustering winds forced me to cling to the branch.

"Well, what does it say?" Tabitha whispered, a few feet behind me.

"It says '*Bring him to hospital.*' "

"Bring *who* to hospital?" Tabitha asked.

Before I could read the rest of the text, we heard the tortured scrape of metal on metal. Looking up, we saw Peak opening an upstairs window. The sight of his evil darkness caused me to instantly look away. And, much worse, to drop my phone.

I lunged forward as my phone fell into empty air. Against all odds, I caught it. Unfortunately, I also fell into empty air. Elbows over butt, I tumbled from the oak tree toward the barbed wire fence below. I had time for just one quick thought: *I'm dead.*

WHAM!

I hit something, another tree limb below. Bouncing off of it, my sunglasses flew, and I fell onto Jack Peak's property, narrowly missing the fence.

I landed on a dirt mound. Wind knocked out of me, I heard Peak shouting something.

I'm dead, I thought again. But then I realized he wasn't yelling at me.

The mound blocked me from his line of sight. Peak threw a handful of bones into his backyard. I couldn't tell if they were animal bones or people bones, but they were definitely bones.

As I hugged the mound and said a prayer for protection, my cell vibrated. Expecting to hear Sandra Morton's voice, I answered. It was her daughter instead.

"Oh, my God, Bertie, are you okay?" Tabitha asked.

"Yes. My face broke my fall." I saw Tabitha perched in the tree above me.

"Don't move," she said. "If you do, the creepy axe murderer will see you. He's looking that way."

"Okay…"

"Oh, no! Your sunglasses are on top of the mound. Quick, grab them."

"You just said don't move!"

"Do it! If Mr. Peak spots those glasses you are *so* dead. Hurry!"

I blindly reached my hand atop the mound.

"No, Bertie, more to the left," Tabitha said.

I searched more to the left.

"Your other left, idiot," she said, chuckling.

Finally, I found my sunglasses. During the fall, one of the arms had snapped off. I tried them on to see if they still worked.

They did. In the corner of my eye, I noticed a dozen little stars orbiting around me. *Great, I have a concussion*, I thought.

Then panic. They weren't stars, they were honeybees with silver auras. And they were flying into a huge beehive attached to the mound I had landed on.

"Tabitha, is Peak looking at me?" I asked in a rapid-fire panic. "I'm sitting near a giant beehive. I'm totally allergic to bees, and I have to get out of here now!"

"Can you make it to the rear of his truck?" she said.

Getting up, a sudden sharp pain shot through me. My left arm was bruised and aching. Still, I had to get away before I got stung. Dashing from the hive and the mound, I zigzagged between various junk piles. Peak's truck was roughly twenty yards away. Over the cell, Tabitha gave me directions from above. "Washing machine, hide behind it." Or "Stop, duck down, he's looking." Or "Run to the woodpile. Go-go-go!"

Finally, I reached the Dodge. I had an escape route to Peak's front gate. All I wanted was to leave that dark and miserable hellhole. But something caught my eye in the backyard. At first, it was hard to see through the property's swirling dark aura. It was like looking through a black sandstorm. Amid the roiling swell of dust and darkness, I spied a tiny dot of gold. It was faint and hidden behind carcasses of rusted snowmobiles.

All at once, my head cleared. Everything made perfect sense. From finding the glasses, to the Girl Scout cookies, even falling out of the tree. Everything that had happened up to now led me to this moment, gazing at Jack Peak's backyard.

"Tabitha, I see something," I reported.

"What do you see?" she asked.

"Hope. A speck of hope."

"What does that mean? What are you telling me?"

"I'm telling you that I know what we have to do. And why we have to do it together."

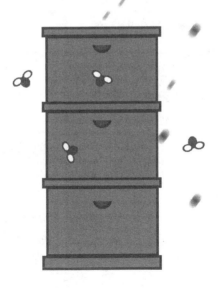

44

The Last Speck of Hope in The World

The golden flicker beckoned me like an enchanted gemstone in a fairy tale or a video game.

Moving closer, I saw paw prints in the dirt, a filthy water bowl, and a chain tied to a railroad spike.

"Mac's dog Cosmo was a terrier, right?" I said to Tabitha, over my cell.

"Yep," she said. "Why are you asking me that question?"

"Cosmo is the speck of hope, Tabitha."

In Peak's yard I saw a dog that matched the photo on the posters Mac and Tabitha had put up around their neighborhood, a fresh batch of flyers every month or two. Or what was left of him. Cosmo's black and white fur was dirty and matted, and missing in spots. Bones protruded from his rail-thin body. His leather collar was hooked to the silver chain. The sight of the poor abused terrier busted my heart into a million pieces.

When Cosmo saw me, he started barking. Not a *go away* kind of bark, but a *save me* bark. In my phone I heard Tabitha's breathless shock.

"It *is* Cosmo. Oh my God, Bertie, he's so skinny!" She was trying not to bawl. "You are right, this is why my mom sent us here. We have to get Cosmo to Mac. It might help him wake up."

Tabitha hissed. "This monster had Cosmo for two years. He stole Mac's dog!"

"And now we are going to steal Cosmo back," I said. "But I just can't go and grab him. Peak will see me. Plus, I can't do much with my left arm. It's all bruised and weird."

"So how are we going to get Cosmo?"

Fast as I could, I told her my idea. A ludicrous two-girl plan.

SCRAPE!

Thirty feet away from me, a glass door slid open.

Big Jack Peak stalked onto his deck, his aura blacker than a crow's wing. I ducked down as he shouted, "Shut up, ya stupid fleabag!" Grabbing a rusty metal garbage can lid, Peak whipped it at Cosmo. The lid clanged against a snowmobile instead. "Not one more bark, hear me?"

Cosmo looked at me like I was his last speck of hope in the world.

Then he barked, as if begging me to take him away from this hellish life. Daggers of red rage shot from Peak's head as he yelled at the dog. "You done did it now!" Snatching an axe from near the back door, Peak started down the porch steps after the helpless but defiant terrier. "Get ready to catch a beating!"

There was no time to waste. I had to move. I ran off.

Cosmo tried to run away too, as the axeman approached. Snatching Cosmo's chain, Peak reeled the yelping dog toward him. Cosmo's paws dug into the dirt, trying to resist. But it was no use, until…

DING-DONG!

Jack Peak stopped tormenting Cosmo. "Who the hell is ringing my doorbell?"

Through grimy windows by the front door, I saw the axe murderer stomping toward me. He still had the axe in his big hands.

It took all of sixty seconds.

The door swung open. The air swirled, and I swallowed a gruesome mouthful of the dark and stormy aura that billowed around the monster.

"Can't you read, little rat?" he said. "What are you doing on my property?"

Pointing the axe blade at NO SOLICITING and NO TRESPASSING signs posted on his front gate, shadowy tendrils twisted out of Peak's body and loomed over me.

I did my best to act natural and unafraid. But it was next to impossible.

The only reason I could get past the hideous taste in my mouth and my overwhelming fear of Jack Peak, was because I was a hundred times more afraid of letting down a beaten-down dog, a wonderful, dying eight-year old boy, his ghost mother, my mom, and my better self.

So rather than run for my life, I stuck to my ridiculous plan.

"Hello, Mr. Peak, today is your lucky and delicious day!" I said, digging out four cookie boxes from my backpack. "On behalf of the Girl Scouts of America, I'd like to thank you for your order."

45

Something Stinks

"I didn't order no stinkin' Girl Scout cookies!" the monster barked.

"Don't be so sure, Mr. Peak," I said, pretending to check my phone for orders.

Glancing to my left, I saw Tabitha carrying out her part of the plan. Hanging off a lower tree branch, she dropped down into Peak's property. Junk piles prevented me from seeing whether she had stuck the landing or it had stuck her.

"Oh, I'm plenty sure!" Peak said. He lowered his dirt-smeared nose inches from mine. Streaks of his black aura snapped at my face like snake heads. "You trying to murder me, little rat?" His breath was so hot and foul it just about fried my eyebrows off. "I'm diabetic! If I eat even one of those dang cookies, I could go into insulin shock."

"Lucky for you, the cookies also make excellent gifts, Mr. Peak, and you'll be glad to know that our Thin Mints are one hundred percent..."

The axe murderer snatched my bruised arm. My insides exploded in agony. I wanted to cry out, but I couldn't. Through the window next to Peak's front door, I spotted Tabitha in the backyard. Cosmo was so overjoyed to see her, he covered her face with wet kisses.

I forced myself to look away, worried that Peak would follow my gaze. We were all going to be dead meat if I couldn't keep the monster distracted. Gritting my teeth, I forced myself to keep smiling. "If Thin Mints aren't your thing, Mr. Peak, our Toffee-Tastic cookies are gluten-free."

He narrowed his eyes at me. "Hold on. I knew I seen you before, little girl!" The monster squeezed my arm so tightly I nearly saw stars. "Last week or so, you was loitering outside my gate!"

"Please stop hurting my arm, Mr. Peak," I said as my legs grew weak and tears spilled out of my eyes. "Or I'll be forced to take back my cookies."

"You was with them lousy Morton kids," he said, pointing the axe. "As I recall, I gave you little rats fair warning. Now, I done caught you red-handed. I got me every legal right to gut you."

CLANG.

A noise in the backyard stopped Peak mid-sentence. Looking over his shoulder, he saw Tabitha trying to free Cosmo from the chain.

To my surprise, Mr. Peak just smiled like he was happy. The monster's teeth were crooked and coated in scum. "Guess you was right, today *is* my lucky day. I got two little rats trying to burgle me! Just one question for you, rat number one, how ya'll gonna steal my damn dog without no key?"

Jangling a key chain on his belt, the Creepy Axe Murderer lived up to his nickname. He reared the axe over his head. "Oh, yeah, I got me every legal right!"

"AHHH!" I screamed in horror.

Peak started to swing his axe down, but for some mysterious reason he stopped doing that as he yelled and cursed up a storm, as if in great pain.

What happened?

I had no idea, until the monster spun around. I finally saw Leon biting Peak's left leg. And Leon was not letting go.

"Get off of me, dang dog!" Swiping at Leon, Peak tripped down his broken front steps. Timbering into his junkyard like a toppled redwood, the monster banged his head on an old sewing machine. THUD!

His eyelids fluttered in a daze.

The monster was down, but not out. I had to move fast. Reaching down, I unsnapped Peak's keychain off of his belt.

"Good boy, Leon, let's go!" Sprinting to the backyard, we found Tabitha still trying to free Cosmo.

"I have Peak's keys," I said, and then I tried to fit a key into Cosmo's lock.

"Where is he, Bertie?" Tabitha said. "Where's Mr. Peak?"

"Leon gave him a time out," I said, trying more keys with shaky hands. And then *click*. The chain fell off Cosmo's collar. Naturally, he licked my face like crazy. He smelled like an old wet rug, but he was glowing brighter than ever.

Until he wasn't. Suddenly, Cosmo's gold aura dimmed.

"Here comes the pain, little rats." Tabitha and I turned and saw Jack Peak thumping toward us, his aura more vile and stormy than ever. Holding his axe, and with blood flowing down his face, he was the ultimate deranged monster.

"You stole my brother's dog!" Tabitha said. "Cosmo belongs to my brother Mac, and we are taking him out of here." Her aura shone crimson and gold. It wasn't rage, it was righteousness. In that light, Tabitha looked like a warrior princess. She looked brave.

Slapping the axe handle against his meaty palm, Peak said, "Ya'll ain't going nowhere!"

Rushing forward, Leon snapped at the axe murderer,

but the monster kicked him away. My eyes went red with outrage. Now I rushed at Peak. Or I started to. Behind him, I saw a silvery cloud of stars buzzing and swarming toward the monster.

A colony of bees. Thousands of tiny bee-stars descended onto Peak like a moving constellation. Pawing at the bees, he writhed and cursed and rolled on the ground as the swarm covered him like a silver glittering blanket.

Not a single bee bothered Cosmo, Leon, Tabitha, or me. Something miraculous was happening. I could sense it, and I hoped Tabitha could, too.

"It's my mom isn't it?" she said, awestruck. "She's directing the bees, Bertie. She's giving us a way out!"

"Then let's take it. C'mon!" I grabbed Leon, and Tabitha picked up Cosmo. Only she didn't seem to want to leave just yet.

"But, my mom… I can feel her. She's definitely here," Tabitha said, her eyes tearing up.

"We don't have much time, Tabitha. Your mom told us to bring Cosmo to the hospital," I said. "Mac needs him!"

And so we ran, sprinting as fast as we could toward the front gate.

Only the monster wasn't done just yet. A truck engine roared behind us. Looking back, I saw Peak behind the wheel of his Dodge, covered in bees. Pounding the gas, he aimed the truck at us. We were trapped with no way out.

Winds stirred, and then a rusty washing machine flew into the air and smashed into the speeding truck. CRASH! Peak drove faster, undeterred, until an old snowmobile flew out of nowhere, smashing his windshield. BANG! He kept going. It seemed like nothing was going to stop the monster from crushing us. Finally, the broken refrigerator where Peak stowed his homemade grain alcohol contraption rocketed against the side of the truck. BOOM! Flames spread over the truck's hood as Peak crashed the burning Dodge into his house.

Tabitha, Leon, Cosmo, and I watched Peak frantically jump out of his truck.

He was *still* coming for us. I will tell you this: there's nothing more dangerous than a wounded bee-stung killer.

But then the silvery star-lit bees swarmed on the axe murderer again. A cursing Peak ran screaming inside his house like a demented bee-covered monster.

I was wrong. It wasn't Mr. Peak's lucky day, after all.

46

Racing to the Hospital

We hadn't run ten yards from the axeman's house, when we spotted the purple Subaru waiting to Uber us away.

"Hello again, ladies!" Miko said, with a grin. "Ready to roll?"

Jumping into the car, Tabitha smiled. "How cool is my mom? It's amazing. It's like she knew everything before it even happened."

I nodded.

"It's amazing, alright. Except for the part where I fell out of the tree and almost got killed ten times."

Miko's grin faltered.

"Yuck-yuck, ladies!" She motioned to Cosmo. "No way is that mangy mutt allowed inside my taxi. He stinks to high heaven." She pointed outside. "Out, get him out!"

"No-no, Cosmo has to come with us," I said. "Miko, I promise we will write you a million-star review, but we are in a huge life or death situation, and we got to get to the hospital, so please-please step on it!"

Miko didn't budge.

"Will you tell everyone you know to buy my kid's cookies?" she asked.

"If you get us to the hospital in time, I'll do even better," I said. "I'll get Tabitha's dad to buy all of your daughter's cookies, Miko, every last box."

"Every box?" she said. "I got like ten cases more in the trunk."

"Go!" I pleaded, while Tabitha shouted, "Drive!"

Away we went. Miko stepped on the gas pedal.

Cosmo stuck his head out of the window, enjoying the new scenery and new scents like a prisoner who had just been released from jail. Tail wagging and pink tongue lolling out of his mouth, he dog-smiled at the world.

Minutes later, Miko skidded to a stop in front of the hospital. Hurrying out of the taxi, I told her Mac's room number so she could sell Girl Scout cookies to Howard, then Tabitha and I sprinted to the front doors.

I held Leon with my good arm. Tabitha clutched stinky Cosmo.

Automatic doors opened. As we raced toward the elevators, we heard a man shouting, "Excuse me! No animals are allowed in this hospital."

Up ahead, I saw it was Neck Tattoo and Muscle Guy Guard. The security guards marched toward us. Time went into slow motion.

Their eyes widened in surprise.

"Whoa, hey," Neck Tattoo said. "It's the Lost and Found girl. That's her!" The guards looked at me like it was Christmas morning. The hunters had finally trapped their prey.

"Grab her!"

47

Taser Fight

"Lost and Found girl? What does that even mean?" Tabitha asked.

"It's a long story," I said.

I couldn't believe this was happening. Fifteen minutes ago, we had escaped from an axe murderer's lair, and now we were about to be arrested by goofy hospital cops.

Watching Neck Tattoo and Muscle Guy Guard approach, I read their auras. Both of them were jacked up, but the colors of their auras told me they were worried. And rightfully so. Last time they saw me, a platoon of empty wheelchairs attacked them.

"This is my brother Mac Morton's dog," Tabitha told the men. "We have to—"

"Zip it!" Neck Tattoo ordered. "You kids are coming with us."

206

I felt something stir in the air. A hint of electricity. There was no time to mess around. Instinctively, I knew what to do.

"No disrespect, gentlemen, but that's not going to work for us," I told the guards. "Here's what's going to happen. My friend and I are taking *these* two dogs into *that* elevator. And you guys are going to pretend you never saw us. Got it?"

"I'll get this one, Tommy, you get the other one." Muscle Guy Guard came at me. "We are hauling you to the Security Office, right now."

"Don't say I didn't warn you," I said.

As Muscle Guy Guard reached out to grab me, the craziest thing happened.

ZZZAAAPPP!!!

Neck Tattoo zapped his partner with roughly thirty thousand volts of electricity from a taser gun he pulled from his belt.

Muscle Guy Guard reared backward in agony, and yanked out a barb stuck to his right arm. "Ow! What the heck are you doing?"

Neck Tattoo looked baffled beyond belief. "I … I honestly don't know."

"It'll only get worse, guys," I said. "Be smart and let us go!"

But Muscle Guy Guard wasn't smart.

When he reached for me again, Neck Tattoo zapped him a second time. The barb stuck to Muscle Guy Guard's shirt and chest.

"Dude, sorry!" Neck Tattoo gaped at Muscles stupidly.

"Apology *not* accepted!" Drawing his own taser, Muscle Guy Guard shot Neck Tattoo. The fight was on. Jagged blue lines of electricity crackled between the two security guards as more barbs flew out from their tasers.

ZZZAAAPPP!!!

ZZZAAAPPP!!!

ZZZAAAPPP!!!

"Wow!" I said, walking with Tabitha to the elevators. "Your mom is electric!"

Tabitha grinned and pressed the UP button.

After the doors opened, we slid inside.

Leon farted, loud and proud. Cosmo answered in kind.

48

Cosmo and Mac

Stepping off the elevator, we saw the Morton gang holding a prayer vigil in the ICU waiting area. Heads lowered, their auras were dense and dark. The colors of lost hope.

Were we too late? A rush of panic swept through me. My chest tightened, and my knees went weak.

"Tabitha, where have you been?" Big Mouth Aunt said, looking up. "I'm sorry, honey, but it's happening. Mac is leaving us."

Tabitha glared at her aunt.

"Get away from me with that loser talk," Tabitha barked. "Not another word. Mac is *not* going anywhere!"

Big Mouth Aunt's mouth slammed shut like a trap door. You could almost hear a metallic clank. Normally, this would've been fun to see, but nothing was normal. So we ignored Big

Mouth Aunt and marched to Mac's room. Two girls and two dogs on a life and death mission. Behind us a nurse shouted, "Excuse me, what are you girls thinking, bringing two smelly dogs in here?" We ignored her too, and kept going.

Tabitha pushed open a door, and carried Cosmo inside the room. I followed, holding Leon.

Not one person noticed us.

Howard held Mac's small hand in his big hands. My mom stood beside them, weepy and sad. Dr. Myles had his nose in a medical chart, seemingly looking for something he might've missed. Still wearing the glasses, I glanced around for Sandra Morton's ghost, but didn't see her.

As I stepped closer, the sight of Mac stole my breath.

He was at death's door. His skin was so pale, he didn't look real. A faint glow seeped from his body. It looked like a sputtering light bulb fading out. I'd seen this exact fading light coming off Sandra Morton in Room 555 just before she died.

Now, Mac was dying in Room 548. Closing my eyes, I said a silent prayer, offering the universe every last watt of my own light to save Mac's life.

"Tabitha?" Howard's voice pulled me back to the room, and the cold reality of Mac's nearing death. "Is that … It can't be … Cosmo?"

"It is, Dad. It's Cosmo," Tabitha said.

"How … Where?" Howard said in disbelief. "Where'd you find him?"

"Mom told Bertie where to look for Cosmo. She wanted us to bring him here."

Tabitha placed Cosmo at the foot of Mac's bed. The dog sniff-sniffed, and his aura brightened like a golden gem. Being near the boy he loved most in the world turned Cosmo the color of joy. Tail wagging, he padded up the bed toward Mac's ashen face.

It was too late to make a difference. A thick blackness had crept into Mac's aura like an oil spill, gobbling up what was left of his light. His heart rate was thirty-eight beats per minute, according to a monitor, and his blood pressure was dropping fast.

"Don't give up, Mac!" Howard said, tears streaming.

"Fight it, Mac," Tabitha said. "You never stopped believing you'd find Cosmo, even after everyone else had given up. He's here with you now, Mac. Cosmo's here!"

Cosmo went to work, licking Mac's face and nuzzling him with his nose like he was trying to nudge him awake. When Mac didn't respond, Cosmo started howling like a wolf.

AWOOOOOOOOOO!

To my surprise, Leon joined in.

AWOOOOOOOOOO!

The howling was haunting and powerful, but it wasn't enough. Mac's vital signs dropped further. His glow fizzled out like the final ember of a once-great fire.

The monitors showed zeroes, and went silent.

People's hands went to their mouths.

Tears fell.

AWOOOOOOOOOO!

Eight-year-old Mac Morton was dead. And I was the one who killed him, not the truck driver. No, that ten-ton weight was on my shoulders alone, pressing down on me and stealing my air.

Dr. Myles dropped the chart and ran out of the room.

"We need a crash cart in here," he shouted. "Code Blue!"

Even though Mac was showing no signs of life, Cosmo didn't give up. The stinky dog kept showering Mac with kisses.

And then it happened: Mac's aura lightened. Gray swirls pushed aside deathly blacks. Tiny gold flecks appeared, and I saw a rolling band of silver. Mac's glow came alive before my eyes. And so did the rest of him. The monitor readouts flashed rising numbers.

Dr. Myles returned with two nurses, and a cart full of machinery and medical supplies. He glanced at Mac, then he gaped at the beeping monitors. "What's happening? Look at the monitors!"

Forty-two beats per minute…

Forty-six beats…

Forty-eight beats…

Fifty-one…

"Keep it going, Mac!" My mom cheered, dripping tears.

"Yes, son, be strong!" Howard said.

"C'mon on, Mac. Come back to us!" Tabitha clapped like we were at a school pep rally.

"Come back, Mac, and your next hundred ice cream cones are on me!" I cheered, too. "And a million Girl Scout cookies, courtesy of your dad."

Brilliant light poured from Mac's body and fingertips like someone had flipped on a switch. The colors were nearly blinding, but it was impossible to turn away from the light. The rush of Mac's radiant colors changed the auras of everyone in the room. Earlier, I had seen this happen with Dr. Myles when his fear had spread to other people like a plague.

Now, I saw the exact opposite. Fear was replaced by dazzling rainbow colors of love and peace and gratitude. Dr. Myles stared at the monitors, awestruck. "His vitals are normalizing!"

And that's when Mac woke up!

Eyelids blinking open, Mac looked right at me. "Bertie, you owe me…" His voice was a scratchy whisper. "… a hundred ice cream cones."

Euphoria.

Rapture.

Ecstasy.

Howard held his son's hand and wept. Dr. Myles examined Mac's eyes with a penlight. Everyone else in the room gathered around the bed and cheered, hugged, kissed, and cried.

Hearing the celebration, Big Mouth Aunt and the other Mortons herded into the room, shouting:

"Woo-hoo!"

"Welcome back, Mac!"

"Hallelujah!"

Over the cheering, I overheard Dr. Myles talking to a nurse. "This is … it's a miracle. I've heard of things like this, but I've never actually witnessed it. I was prepared to call Mac's time of death. It was basically over until the girls brought those dirty dogs in here."

"Cosmo, I knew you'd come back to me. I just knew it," Mac said. Though tired and weak, the miracle boy hugged his lost dog. "Whoa, Cosmo, you need a bath."

Turning to his dad and sister, Mac said, "Hi, Daddy. Hi, Tabitha."

"Oh, Mac!" Tabitha said, while Howard melted like ice cubes under a heat lamp. "We missed you so much!"

"I know you guys missed me 'cause I saw you here," Mac said. "I saw lots of things. I even saw Mommy."

The room went quiet as Sunday morning.

"You saw Mommy?" Tabitha said, speaking in a hush. "Where, Mac?"

"I was in a dark place, and I couldn't get out." Mac was sleepy, and his voice trailed off. "She told me that you and Bertie were going to rescue Cosmo for me. Mommy told me it wasn't my time ... and that I needed to return to the living world. I had so many people who loved me and so many things ... I needed to do."

"Mom was right, buddy." Howard smiled, and sniffled. "You have lots and lots yet to do. And years and years left to live."

"Dad, I'm not sure what this means ... but Mommy said she likes the new love song you and Bertie's mom sing to each other," Mac said, looking at his father and my mom. "So keep singing it."

Howard slung his arm around my mom. What happened next? We are talking a hospital flooding tear-fest, folks. Mom and Howard cried as they pulled Tabitha and me into their embrace. Together, we held Mac, Cosmo, and Leon.

All of us cried and cried and cried. The nurse and Dr. Myles, too. And Howard's relatives.

215

"Bertie."

I heard a familiar voice. My father had arrived. It was time for me to go home to North Carolina.

I dabbed at my eyes with my shirt. When I whipped around so I could throw a smile at my dad, the sunglasses flew off. The lenses shattered.

49

Decision Time

A half hour after Mac's awakening, Dad took me to a pizza place on Chestnut Avenue, not far from the hospital. Throughout the meal, I sneaked looks through the broken lenses of my sunglasses. What was left of them, anyway, which wasn't much.

The magic was gone. Sandra Morton's ghost was gone. And Better Bertie was gone, too. Losing Better Bertie hurt the most. I was on my own.

Better Bertie warned me that things were going to happen that I would not understand. But she also said when the moment was right, it would all make sense. This was the moment when everything made sense to me, inside the pizza restaurant with my dad, sitting in a booth by the window.

Here it goes.

Without Better Bertie nudging me to be a better person and to see people and the world differently, I would've never found the courage to go on the crazy-dangerous mission to rescue Cosmo from the axe murderer. Mac and Cosmo don't reunite. Mac never wakes up from the coma. He *dies*. Howard and Mom break up, and Mom and I move back to North Carolina. The wound of Mac's death and my role in it festers and burns and itches for the rest of our lives. Never completely heals.

And that's why Sandra Morton engineered the entire deal with the hoodoo sunglasses and Better Bertie. I had to become a better person before I could be brave enough and decent enough and selfless enough to do whatever it took to save her son, Mac, and keep him in the living world, even if it meant putting my own life at risk.

Somehow, Sandra saw each puzzle piece ahead of time, and all the gaping holes that needed to be filled in if Mac was going to survive. And so she left behind her sunglasses so I would use them to find my higher self, to see auras and shooting stars, and other proof that the universe was paying attention to me and to Mac. But only if I kept my eyes wide open, and traced the lines of connection between people, places, and events, and even different years, like when I time-traveled in Room 555.

It's a two-way relationship. Ignore the universe, and it

218

might ignore you back. And it's a trust issue, I think. Trust the universe, and miracles become possible. Including the absolute miracle of a sweet and mischievous eight-year-old boy coming back to life, in good part because of the boundless love of a dirty and stinky dog.

But it wasn't simply about Mac waking up. It was about healing all of us: Howard, Tabitha, Mom, me, and even skinny-to-his-bones Cosmo. And Leon, who now had a dog friend to play with. Who knows, maybe Sandra Morton did some self-healing while she was in Altoona. I'd like one more chat with her, but I don't think that will ever happen.

"What's the story with those busted sunglasses?" Dad said after wiping tomato sauce off his mouth with a paper napkin.

I wanted to tell my dad every crazy, spooky thing that had happened to me, but I couldn't—it was too soon. Besides, we had more immediate matters to discuss. Even though Mac was out of the woods, Dad still wanted me and Leon to return home with him to North Carolina. And a huge part of me wanted to go, but it felt like the selfish part.

Thanks to Mac coming back to life, Mom and Howard had an opportunity to save their relationship. A second chance to be happy again. How could I ruin that? If I left Altoona, Mom would leave, too. We were a package deal, so the better part of me knew I should stay. Plus, I really wanted to help Mac get back on his feet. So that's what I told my dad, that I needed to stay in Pennsylvania for a while. Family members, current and future, were counting on me, and I was tired of letting people down.

"You sure about this, Peach Pie?" Dad asked.

"No," I said. "But I need to do it anyway."

My dad wasn't giving up. He was a winning attorney, and he wouldn't go down without a battle. I could tell he really wanted me to come with him, especially when he started using his cross-examination tactics. "Remember our phone calls and video chats, Bertie? You said Howard's house was haunted. You told me you were seeing ghosts, did you not?"

I silently shrugged.

"Don't just shrug, give me an answer," he said. "Do you see ghosts, or not?"

"Ghosts? I wish." I said.

"What's that supposed to mean?" Dad asked.

I didn't want to lie.

Standing up, I gave my dad a hug. "It means I love you, Daddy."

He hugged me tightly. I smelled his minty aftershave and the goop he puts in his hair. "I love you too, Fluffy Stuff," my dad said.

My eyes welled with tears. In my heart I already missed him.

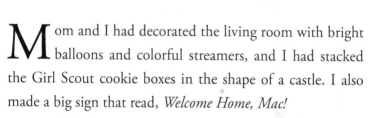

50

Sea of Stars

Mom and I had decorated the living room with bright balloons and colorful streamers, and I had stacked the Girl Scout cookie boxes in the shape of a castle. I also made a big sign that read, *Welcome Home, Mac!*

Mac's face lit up as he speed-crutched his way through the front door with Howard and Tabitha. It had been a month since the accident, so Mac's right leg and arm were still in casts. Somehow, that had made him faster. No joke. The kid could outrun a rocket.

Even though Mac's recovery was considered a miracle, Dr. Myles suggested we take it slow during Mac's first few days home. The party was limited to Mac, Howard, Mom, Tabitha, Cosmo, Leon, and me.

"Wow! Look at all those cookies!" Mac said, hugging

Cosmo. His dog jumped up and down so high I thought he might crash through the ceiling.

"Believe it or not, buddy, your dad ponied up for every cookie here," I said, motioning to the castle. "Three-hundred and eighty-five boxes worth of sugary delights."

"Three-hundred and eighty-four boxes," Howard said, patting his belly.

"More like three-eighty-three," Mom told Mac. "Well, actually, three hundred and eighty-two boxes. Sorry, but I'm a sucker for the S'mores. They're criminally delicious!"

"You guys are terrible!" Tabitha said. "But since we're being honest, let's round it down to three-eighty, even."

Mac felt good enough to join in the fun. Ripping open a box of Tagalongs, the little guy shouted like a natural-born auctioneer. "Do I hear three-seventy-nine?"

We all rocked with laughter. The dogs barked and wagged their tails. It was only a small welcome home party, but there had never been a happier one.

A short while later, Howard and Mom joined hands and announced they were moving their wedding to Thanksgiving so Mac could complete his physical therapy. Howard asked if that would be okay with us kids.

"We are a family," he said, "and this is a family decision."

It was more than okay. I mean, I'm not sure we felt like

a family just yet, especially me and Tabitha, but we were stoked for them. A tragedy had pushed Mom and Howard's relationship to the brink of oblivion, and they had come back even more committed to each other.

Yay for Mom and Howard, right?

The news made Tabitha pensive about something. Taking me aside, she whispered, "Look, Bertie, I know your sunglasses are broken, but I've been wondering, have you seen my mom again?" She gave me a crooked but hopeful smile. She wanted me to say "yes."

"No. I'm sorry, Tabitha," I said. "I haven't seen her since the day the glasses broke. The day of Mac's miracle."

Her smile faded.

"Yeah, I figured you would have said something if you saw her. It was stupid of me to ask. It's just that from the moment we brought Mac home, I've felt my mom's presence. I don't know how, but even now I feel it."

"Your mom is here," I said, glancing outside to see the moon and sun sharing the twilight sky. "Meet me on the roof in ten minutes."

Ten minutes later, we stood on the Mortons' roof. Twilight had turned into night. The full moon shone bright in the night sky. I was hoping Tabitha would shine, too. She motioned to the backyard, confused.

"You did this today?" she said.

"With help from my mom, when you guys were picking up Mac at the hospital. I asked Howard if would be okay, and he said he thought it would be fine."

"It's perfect," Tabitha said.

We shared a smile.

Earlier, Mom and I had planted dozens of lavender flowers, the same kind of flower Sandra Morton had loved sharing with Tabitha and Mac. The flowers' soothing scent filled the air. And, in the brilliant moonlight, the purple and blue petals glowed like a sea of stars. It stole our breath in the best of ways.

Standing there in silence, Tabitha and I took in the galaxy of earthbound stars and all they represented. And they represented so much. Neither of us spoke a word for five or six minutes. Then, finally, she turned to me, her voice soft and generous.

"Bertie?" Tabitha said. "The girl you told me you saw before, the girl who went away?"

"You mean Better Bertie?" I said.

She nodded. "I'm not so sure she ever left."

"What do you mean?"

Tabitha measured her words carefully. "This might sound strange coming from me, but I think … you became her. I think you are Better Bertie, Bertie."

It did sound strange, coming from Tabitha. I stared at her in shock.

"Did I say something wrong?" she asked.

"No," I said, my voice catching in my throat. "Truth is, that's got to be the nicest thing anyone has ever said to me."

Feeling salty water filling my eyes, I hugged Tabitha close so she wouldn't see me cry. Patting my shoulder, she said, "Don't get used to it, Bertie. I'm usually a big meanie."

I laughed, and remembered what my great-aunt Tillie said about the difference between heaven and hell. Now, I can't say Pennsylvania was exactly heaven on Earth, but it sure had its heavenly moments. Like there on the roof with Tabitha, the moon shining down on the lavender Mom and I had planted in remembrance of Sandra Morton.

My mom was right. A fresh start was exactly what we needed, but it took me a lot longer to realize it. I needed help from a desperate ghost, a smarty-pants doppelganger, a mangy dog, and the *entire universe* before I saw the truth.

I was wrong about something else. It was a mistake when I thought that Tabitha and I weren't family yet. We were a mishmash family, but a family nonetheless.

We were sisters.

Hearing music coming from downstairs, Tabitha and

I left the roof so we could rejoin Mac's party. As I slipped through the attic window, Tabitha said, "Careful. You don't want to bump your gigantic melon-head."

For the first time in my life, I had no snarky comeback.

Joining my mom and Howard and Mac in the living room, I wondered if Better Bertie and Ghost Mom were silently keeping watch over us somewhere. Were they looking through a magic mirror, or seeing us by some other supernatural means? Not just that night, but also in the days that would follow.

51

Epilogue

Wait! Don't leave. There are a few more things you need to know. It will be worth it, I promise.

During the bus ride to school, four boys seated in the back are having a loud argument about Jack Peak. Apparently, he left Altoona under mysterious circumstances. No one has seen him since the illegal grain alcohol still on his property exploded and set his truck and his house on fire. All sorts of wicked rumors are flying about. "What *really* made the monster leave town?" one of the boys asks.

Sitting next to me, Tabitha gives me a knowing smile and a fist bump as the bus pulls in front of Washington Middle School. I have to wonder if we will ever see the crazed axe murderer again.

As we climb off the bus to start our first day of seventh

grade, Tabitha cheers me on. "You're going to do great today, Bertie, I know it."

"Thanks," I say, hiding my panic. I know I'm not like the other students, and I never will be. And Tabitha knows it, too. Honestly, I'm glad for that. I just hope I don't stick out like a mouse in a python parade. The weirdo new girl kids make fun of.

Minutes later, the tardy bell is about to ring, and I still can't find my homeroom. Granted, my mind is a bit overwhelmed because something mind-blowing is going on. I was just sideways glancing at a cute boy passing by, when WHAM, it happened. No, I did not fall madly in love with the kid.

I saw his aura. Really.

Blowing out a thunderstruck breath, I rub my eyes and look again. Yep, I see the boy's aura, clashing shades of purple and green. I quickly realize that if I squinch my eyes, I can see certain kids' auras, just like when I wore the hoodoo sunglasses. But I don't have the glasses.

How can this be? This is *not* cool. This is my first day of school. Hey, universe! Cut me some slack already!

Then it gets worse.

I see two wolves. One has icy blue diamond eyes, and the other wolf owns hot red ruby eyes. The wolves are gigantic, at

228

least fifteen feet tall. They are painted on a school wall. Above their heads are the words FIGHT, WOLF PACK, FIGHT!

Turns out the Wolf Pack is the official mascot for Washington Middle School. I'm pretty sure this is no coincidence. Because things get even more strange.

Suddenly, my hair stands straight up. My breath catches, and I've got goose pimples on top of other goose pimples. I hear a crow cawing outside.

Oh man! Is Sandra Morton back? I don't think so. Something about this woo-woo moment feels different.

"Bertie Blount?" says a voice behind me. Whipping around I see a girl, twelve or thirteen. She's strangely dressed, like she jumped out of Nick at Nite rerun of *Little House On the Prairie*. For some reason she has no aura, just a spooky glimmer.

Then it hits me—she's dead. The girl is a ghost. You've got to be kidding me! Another ghost! Apparently, I'm a ghost magnet. Apparently, I'm the only one who can see the ghost girl. So I do what any sane kid would do. I act like she's not there.

BAARRRRRRIIINNNG!

The tardy bell rings. I hurry to my homeroom, realizing I still have no idea where I'm going. The ghost girl hovers beside me step for step. "I lost my sister, Ivy, and was told you could help me find her," she says, touching my arm and giving me the heebie-jeebies.

Great. First a missing dog, now a missing sister. Am I the supernatural Lost and Found girl or something? I keep walking and pretend to be oblivious. By now, the hallway is nearly empty. I'm lost *and* late.

"Bertie, I know you can see me and hear me," the ghost girl says. "I was sent to you specifically."

Ugh. I guess I have to deal with her. "Why would Sandra Morton send you to me?" I ask, giving her an angry *go away* look.

The ghost girl shakes her head, confused.

"Your great-aunt Tillie sent me. She said you have the gift. Which you clearly do since you are talking to me."

A thousand thoughts collide in my mind. No one in my family has seen Tillie in nearly two years. I don't know where she's living or even if she's alive. She just disappeared.

I turn a corner and nearly crash into Principal Culpepper. He's about forty-five, or fifty. He has a full head of unlikely brown hair, and a menacing black aura. Narrowing his eyes, he asks, "Why aren't you in class, Miss Blount?"

"I'm a little bit lost," I say. "I'm looking for my homeroom."

Principal Culpepper glances at my schedule sheet, and points down the hall to Room 33. "I read your file this morning," he says. "You were a troublemaker at your old school. We don't abide rabble-rousers at Washington Middle School. You need to change your ways, or we will be seeing a lot of each other this year."

I put on a smile so sweet I'm practically spraining my face.

"Actually, sir, I'm embracing change. Change is my new best friend." I spot the ghost girl rolling her glowing eyes. I bolt away from the dead girl and her judgy attitude, and from Principal Culpepper's dark, butterfly net aura: I'm the butterfly in that image. I have become a fierce protector of my glow.

Before I get to my homeroom, things get spooky. The air moans and stirs into hurricane-force winds. We are talking super-crazy stuff, guys.

WHAM! The screaming winds pin me to a wall as WHOOSH! WHOOSH! WHOOSH! posters, banners, and signs rip free and fly all about the hallway. CLANG! CLANG! CLANG! Locker doors open and shut at one hundred miles per hour. SMASH! A framed photo of Principal Culpepper crashes to the floor, shattering glass.

Meanwhile, Culpepper's screaming, "Tornado! Take cover!" THWISH! His toupee flies off his head, and I see the shiniest bald head in the universe. For a nanosecond I think,

Wow, does he polish that dome, or what?

Coming to my senses, I realize what's going on. I call out to the ghost girl. "Okay-okay, message delivered. I will help you find your missing sister. Please stop the windstorm."

The new ghost smiles and vanishes. The spooky winds stop churning, the flying debris falls to the floor, and order is restored. Well, sort of. I pat down my wild hair and look back at Principal Culpepper, who is refitting the toupee onto his head and giving me a suspicious gaze. "I don't know what just happened here," he says. "But I will be keeping a close eye on you, Miss Blount."

Unable to stop myself, I say, "Might as well use both eyes so the other one doesn't get jealous, sir." Before he can answer, I turn for my homeroom.

Approaching Room 33, I take a deep breath. If seeing auras and ghosts and Lord knows what else is what my life has become, then I better be okay with it. Who knows, maybe being the school weirdo will actually be kind of cool. I mean, if you're just another sheep in the flock, all you ever see are a bunch of furry butts in front of you, right?

At the very least I know this to be true: Things are about to get really-really interesting. "Here we go," I say, opening the door and stepping inside the classroom and into the next phase of my big, spooky, wonderful life.

Ocelot Emerson

Ocelot Emerson is the freakish result of a mad scientist's experiment gone horribly wrong. Born half magnificent cat, half malicious human, Ocie escaped from the secret International Prison For Wayward Creatures, and into a deep dark woods, only to be captured by a pack of ravenous ghost wolves. In a stroke of good fortune, the Great Spirit Wolves set aside their natural disdain for all things feline and accepted the cat person into their pack, where they taught Ocie how to hunt and tell bizarre yet heartwarming tales. *Bertie's Book of Spooky Wonders* is Ocelot's first novel aimed at feral and phenomenally gifted children. That means you, kid!

CONNECT WITH US

Find more books like this at http://www.Month9Books.com

Facebook: www.Facebook.com/Month9Books
Instagram: https://instagram.com/month9books
Twitter: https://twitter.com/Month9Books
Tumblr: http://month9books.tumblr.com/
YouTube: www.youtube.com/user/Month9Books
Georgia McBride Media Group: www.georgiamcbride.com

OTHER MONTH9BOOKS TITLES YOU MIGHT LIKE

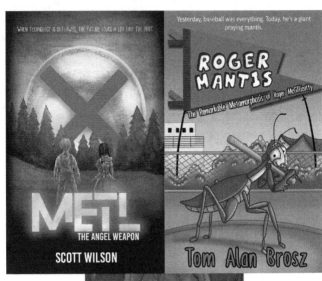